SPECIAL MESSAGE TO READERS

THE ULVERSCROFT FOUNDATION

Yo   ion

Ev   ou
w   or

THE ULVERSCROFT FOUNDATION
The Green, Bradgate Road, Anstey
Leicester LE7 7FU, England
Tel: (0116) 236 4325

website: ft.com

D1493930

Kerry Tombs was born in Smethwick, near Birmingham. After a career in teaching in both England and Australia he moved to Malvern, where he became a local genealogist, lecturer and bookseller. He currently lives in Ludlow, Shropshire.

THE PERSHORE POISONERS

1890: In the Worcestershire market town of Pershore, at Talbots' Lodging House, a recently arrived guest dies in mysterious circumstances. Detective Inspector Samuel Ravenscroft and his colleague, Constable Tom Crabb, are called in to investigate, and are presented with accusations that the dead man was poisoned — a theory borne out by circumstantial evidence. Then a second guest is killed: arsenic is suspected in both deaths, and the policemen's enquiries begin to unearth long-buried secrets. Meanwhile, an old case from Ravenscroft's past threatens to cast a shadow over the present . . .

Books by Kerry Tombs
Published by Ulverscroft:

THE LEDBURY LAMPLIGHTERS
THE DROITWICH DECEIVERS

KERRY TOMBS

THE PERSHORE POISONERS

Complete and Unabridged

ULVERSCROFT
Leicester

First published in Great Britain in 2014 by
Robert Hale Limited
London

First Large Print Edition
published 2015
by arrangement with
Robert Hale Limited
London

A catalogue record for this book is available
from the British Library.

ISBN 978–1–4448–2474–2

Published by
F. A. Thorpe (Publishing)
Anstey, Leicestershire

Set by Words & Graphics Ltd.
Anstey, Leicestershire
Printed and bound in Great Britain by
T. J. International Ltd., Padstow, Cornwall

This book is printed on acid-free paper

To Joan, Samuel and Zoe
For all their support and encouragement
over the years

Contents

Prologue

Pimlico, London 1870

'You know that I am perfectly innocent of this crime. Why must you continue with these infernal questions?'

The policemen remained silent.

'I keep telling you I am not responsible for the death of my poor wife. Why don't you believe me?' pleaded the young man looking across the table at the uniformed officer.

'If you would just answer some more of our questions, Captain Quinton, we would be obliged.'

'Confound you, Inspector,' sighed the man leaning back in the chair and staring up at the grey ceiling of the small, uninviting room.

'How long were you and your wife married, sir?' asked the policeman mopping his sweating brow with a large brown handkerchief, and coughing as he did so.

'I've told you three times already. My wife and I had only been married for three months.'

'Make a note of the good captain's answers, constable,' instructed the questioner addressing the young man standing by the door. 'We

1

may need to produce them in evidence.'

'Yes sir.'

'Now then, when did you and your wife move to Pimlico?'

'Shortly after we were married.'

'When did your wife first become unwell?'

'About three weeks ago. She complained of severe pains in her stomach. She was also violently sick in the night.'

'And what did you do, sir?' asked the inspector leaning forwards and coughing noisily into his handkerchief.

'I called for Doctor Cranford. He came and attended my wife. His conclusion was that she must have eaten something which had disagreed with her.'

'And what happened next, sir?'

'Well he prescribed some medicine for my wife, Charlotte, and advised her to remain in bed for a few days until she recovered.'

'And did your wife make a recovery, sir?'

'She appeared to rally after two or three days, but then the illness returned with the same symptoms. I again called for Doctor Cranford. He treated her and said that we were to feed her on a light gruel until she recovered.'

'But your wife did not recover, did she, sir?' said the policeman before sneezing twice into the handkerchief.

'No. She seemed to fall into a decline. She

was unable to keep down any food for more than a few minutes. I was desperate, Inspector Robertson. I could not understand it. Believe me when I tell you that I would have done anything to save her,' replied Quinton earnestly.

'Can you tell me what happened yesterday, sir, if you please,' asked Robertson before repeating the sneeze.

'Good heavens man, can't you take something for that cold?'

'It's not a cold sir, it's a condition I have. There is no cure. Now if you will kindly answer the question, sir, I should be obliged.'

'It was shortly before three o'clock in the morning. Rachel, the maid, woke me and told me that her mistress was in great pain. I hastily dressed and went into her room. It was dreadful. My wife was screaming out in agony, clutching her stomach and crying out that she was dying. I had never seen her look so deathly white.'

'Very distressing no doubt,' sniffed Robertson.

'We did all that we could to comfort her. I held her in my arms, as she passed away,' replied the young man burying his face in his hands. 'I'm sorry. I cannot go on. This is all so upsetting. Can I have some water?'

'Constable, give the captain a glass of water,' instructed Robertson sneezing into his handkerchief once more.

The young policeman poured out the water from a flagon, and handed it to the distressed man. Robertson leaned back in his chair and studied the man as he swallowed the liquid.

'Thank you. I am sorry. Is there anything else I can help you with?'

'What do you think was the cause of your wife's illness, Captain Quinton?'

'I don't know. I only wish I did, then I could have saved her. It could have been something she inherited from her family I suppose, or a reaction to something she had eaten,' replied Quinton recovering his composure.

'You say that you and your wife had only been married for three months. Where did you first meet your wife, sir?'

'At Pershore in Worcestershire. We were staying at the same hotel.'

'What were you doing there sir?'

'I was spending a few days there on holiday. Why do you ask these questions? It is no concern of yours as to how my wife and I met. All this is becoming irritating, inspector. I think I have answered enough of your questions. Now if you will excuse me, I must attend to the arrangements for my wife's funeral,' said Quinton rising from his chair.

'Just one moment, sir. Constable if you please,' said the detective sneezing once more before addressing his younger colleague.

4

The policeman reached into his pocket and handed his superior a small book.

'What is that?' enquired Quinton.

'A diary, sir, written by your late wife.'

'What? I don't understand,' said Quinton looking down uneasily at the item on the table. 'Where did you get that?'

'We found the diary concealed between a number of items in the drawer of your wife's bedside cabinet. Were you aware, sir, that your wife kept a diary?'

'No, of course not. You made a search of my wife's effects? This is intolerable, sir. You have no right to be prying into my wife's affairs. Good God man, have you no feelings, or compassion, at all? My wife has just died!' shouted Quinton whilst reaching out for the book.

'Just one moment sir,' said Robertson taking hold of the work, before banging it down on the desk. 'We have every right, sir. A young innocent lady struck down in the very prime of her life, for no apparent reason. Dead in the middle of the night. I would say that that more than encourages us in our investigations, sir. Constable, perhaps you would care to read aloud from the deceased's diary. I am sure that Captain Quinton will find the entries most enlightening.'

'This is not to be borne, inspector. I will report this gross violation of privacy to your superior.

Now I suggest you give me that diary at once man,' demanded Quinton rising from his seat.

'Constable, if you would,' instructed Robertson.

'From where, sir?' enquired the young policeman.

'From the young lady's arrival in Pershore. Do take a seat, captain. I am sure that if you are innocent in your wife's death, as you say you are, then you will have nothing to fear from your wife's words.'

'Damn you, man,' snapped Quinton glaring at the detective before resuming his seat.

The constable began reading aloud from the diary —

7 July

Arrived in Pershore this afternoon by the early coach from Oxford. Quite why I have come to this place, I cannot really comprehend. The coach stopped to change horses at the Angel, and as I had little inclination, or desire, to continue the journey to Worcester, I enquired whether they had rooms to let, and have taken one at the front of the building for a few days. Since the death of my poor, beloved Albert it is as if my life has come to an end. Hardly a day goes by when I do not think of how our lives would have been so complete together, but it was not to be. Oh, why did Albert have to go to India? To die in an unknown foreign land, and to leave me so bereft is cruel! Now I am alone, and know not what I am to do with the remainder of my poor life.

8 July
Did not really want to leave my hotel room this morning and had no desire to venture out and explore the town. They say Pershore is a pretty place with some fine buildings, and an abbey of some importance, but although I can see signs of life in the town square from my bedroom window, it fails to attract me. Just lay on the bed all day thinking of my dear Albert, and what our lives might have been.

9 July
My chambermaid, a young whimsical kind of girl, could not understand why I had no desire to venture out to explore the town. I explained to her that I had not been well, and that all I desired was complete rest and to be left alone with my thoughts. I do wish that these people would not seek to impose their desires upon one.

10 July

Have visited the ancient abbey at last. I was not sure that I wanted to leave the sanctuary of my room; I am content with my own company and require no other, but the maid spoke of it again, and gave me an odd look, so I gave in rather than have people think I am strange, or mad!

And what a fine building it is! I stood outside for some minutes not knowing whether I should venture inside. The choir boys were singing Evensong when I entered, and for a moment as I stood there it seemed that everything in my past life had slipped away. And then a strange thing happened. As I turned to leave I accidentally dropped my umbrella on the floor, and before I could bend down to recover it, I found that another had retrieved it for me. A tall, thin gentleman, dressed entirely in black, smiled briefly as he bowed and handed the umbrella back to me. I thanked him, and was about to move away when he enquired whether we had met before. I told him that we had not. Then he said he thought he had seen me the other night in the dining room of my hotel, and yes it appears that he is a guest at the same establishment. He then apologized for his intrusion and quickly made his way out of the building. What a peculiar thing to have happened.

11 July

After writing those words yesterday I had quite expected to see the mysterious stranger at dinner that evening, but it was not to be. And then this morning as I walked along the main street of the town whom should I see coming towards me but the same gentleman I had encountered in the abbey yesterday afternoon! We exchanged a few words of recognition. I asked if he was still resident at the hotel as I had not seen him at dinner the previous evening, to which he replied that he had been called away on urgent business, which had prevented him from dining there — and then he asked me if I would care to dine with him that evening, seeing as we were both staying at the same hotel. I considered this suggestion rather improper, especially as we had only met once before, and anyway I had no desire to converse with anyone at the present, and so I declined his invitation.

12 July

Encountered my stranger again this morning who was standing outside the hotel when I walked out. Most apologetic for his behaviour yesterday. Had not wished to cause any offence. I told him that none had been taken.

Then he asked if I might assist him in a task which he was about to undertake. It seems that an aunt of his had written to him that very day asking him to purchase some lace handkerchiefs for her, and that he was quite at a loss as to what he should choose, and that if I could possibly advise him in any way regarding this purchase, he would be eternally in my debt. I was so taken aback by this unexpected demand that my first inclination was to refuse, and quickly make my way back inside the hotel, but he looked so sad and seemed so much at a loss, that I could not refuse, and so it was that we visited one or two of the local shops in an attempt to complete his errand. I must say that I have never been asked by a stranger before to assist him in such a manner! Thirty minutes later the deed had been done. My stranger introduced himself as a Captain Quinton. He thanked me most profusely for my assistance and helpful advice, and then we went our own separate ways. What an unusual thing to have happened!

13 July
No sign of Captain Quinton today! I'm somewhat relieved.

14 July

I was on my way into dinner tonight when whom should I encounter, but Captain Quinton. He said that he had sent the lace handkerchiefs to his aunt, who had just written to say how pleased she was with them. He was most grateful for my guidance, and said that he would be extremely grateful, and how could he possibly repay me for such kindness? I told him that I had been pleased to be of assistance to him, and that there was no need for him to repay me. However he was most insistent that he would like to be of service to me. He said that he intended visiting the nearby town of Ledbury the next day, and that if I would care to accompany him on this excursion I would be most welcome. Well I was taken aback by this proposal, but he looked so sad that it seemed churlish to refuse. Now that I have written these words I am beginning to regret my hasty decision. Perhaps I will send a message in the morning to say I am unwell.

15 July

Well, in the event I did not send that message and have just returned from a wonderful day's excursion to Ledbury. Captain Quinton had hired a chaise, no less, complete with groom. The weather was fine, warm sunshine with a gentle breeze, but not unpleasantly hot. Ledbury is a fine town indeed, with some old buildings and an interesting ancient market place.

We walked up a narrow cobbled street to view the church, where a local guide showed us around the building, pointing out all the interesting features. Then Captain Quinton said that we should partake of some refreshment at one of the local inns. Although it was such a pleasant occasion, poor Captain Quinton came over suddenly quite sad, and at one point I almost thought that he was going to cry. I must say that I felt very uneasy, and wished that I had not been so bold as to have undertaken such an excursion with a gentleman who was so unknown to me. Then the captain apologized for his unhappy state. It appears that poor Captain Quinton's wife died of smallpox the previous year, and that he has been left quite alone in the world — this day had been the first day in which he had obtained some relief from his unhappy state. He hoped I would understand. I explained to him that I too had recently lost someone who had been close to me. It seems that we had both come to Pershore to seek some relief from the situations in which we had found ourselves. We are like two little orphans who have lost our way. Poor Captain Quinton. As we drove back to Pershore, he said very little, and I must say that I was quite relieved when we returned to the hotel.

July 16
I lay in bed last night going over the events of the day, and it must have been three in the morning before I finally went to sleep. Upon coming downstairs this morning the first person I met in the hallway was Captain Quinton, who appeared to be in quite an agitated condition. He was most insistent that we breakfast together, and once we had been seated, he apologized earnestly for his behaviour yesterday. He had not wanted to burden me with the news of his wife's death. I told him that I quite understood, and that I had not been offended in any way by his conduct. With this he seemed quite satisfied. Then he suggested that there was a performance of *The Messiah* that evening in the abbey and he would be honoured if I would accompany him.

Have just returned from the abbey. What a wonderful evening. *The Messiah* has always been one of my favourite choral works and all the performers gave a spirited rendition. Then whilst we were taking some refreshment in the interval, Captain Quinton told me of his former military career, and it seems that both the captain and my beloved Albert were both members of the same regiment in India. What an amazing coincidence! I was quite taken aback, and the more that Captain Quinton talked of his army days, the more it seemed that he was bringing me ever closer to Albert.

17 July
Captain Quinton, or Charles as he now insists on my addressing him, took me to see the scenery at Symonds Yat today. What a beautiful landscape! As I looked down into the valley at the meandering river, I believed that today was the first day this year that I had been truly happy. Afterwards we partook of some refreshment in Ross-on-Wye, a most agreeable town. The journey back to Pershore was quite charming. Charles is becoming a most pleasant companion, and it seems that my presence has also brought some respite from his suffering.

22 July
Almost five days since my last entry! I have been so occupied accompanying dear Charles on a number of excursions to Worcester and

Malvern, and dining out each evening, that I have not had time to take up my pen. I could not believe that life could be so pleasant once more. At Malvern we hired some donkeys at St Ann's Well which took us up the steep winding paths to the very top of the Beacon, from where we looked down on all the countryside for miles around.

I must say that I am growing quite fond of Charles, and enjoy his company more and more. He is quite handsome in appearance, and is always immaculately dressed, and never without a flower in the buttonhole of his coat.

24 July
I am in a complete state of uncertainty and disarray! This evening over dinner, Charles announced that he had to return to London the following afternoon. Apparently he has a number of business affairs there that require his most urgent attention, and he does not believe that he will return to Pershore for quite a long time. I became very sad on hearing this news — then quite suddenly he grasped my hand, and proposed to me! I was absolutely taken aback!

He said that after his wife had died he had come to believe that he would never find true happiness again, but that during these past days I had brought such joy into his life that he could not bear it if we were to go our separate ways. Seeing that I was startled by his announcement, he apologized if he had been forward in expressing his feelings, and he quite understood if I would like some time to consider his proposal and give him my answer tomorrow.

Oh dear, what am I to do? I have enjoyed Charles's company so much over these days, and the thought of his leaving the day after next, and my never seeing him again, is too much to bear. I believe we could make each other so happy. We are both alone in this world. But what am I to do? To accept his offer would be a kind of betrayal of the love I once had for dear Albert. No, I must decline his offer — and that will be an end to it.

25 July
Captain Quinton and I are engaged to be married!!!!

I had quite made up my mind to refuse him this morning, but when I saw him striding up and down the hall and looking so anxious and forlorn, my heart went out to him, and I knew then that if we were to go our separate ways we would be denying

16

ourselves true happiness.

Charles then held me quite close, and said that this day would be the first of many days filled with such warmth and light.

As he has to leave later today, he asked whether I would accompany him to London, where we may be married as soon as possible. How can I explain my joy?

8 August
I cannot believe that two weeks have gone by since my last entry, but my life has been so eventful and filled with such love and happiness that to put pen to paper would have seemed an intrusion.

I am now Mrs Quinton! Charles and I were married at a little church in Pimlico, where we have secured rooms in one of the most delightful Georgian houses in one of the squares, overlooking a small pleasant garden. I have been quite busy buying things for our home, and seeing that everything is just right for when Charles returns from the City every evening. Charles has engaged a maid to see to our every need. She is called Rachel. I shall be quite spoiled. I have never been so happy. I believe we are quite content.

10 August

Awoke yesterday evening with a terrible pain inside my stomach, and being violently sick. Charles was most attentive, and called for the doctor. It seems I have eaten something which has proved disagreeable to me. Doctor Cranford has prescribed some medicines for me, and instructs me to only eat a little gruel until I am better. Was feeling much better this afternoon to write these words.

11 August

Feeling much improved today. Charles says I must stay in bed for a day or so until I am completely well. The dear man, he is such a comfort to me.

15 August

Today was the first day that I have ventured out since my illness. We walked down to the river and sat in the little park there enjoying the warm sunshine and admiring the views.

18 August

I asked Charles this morning why we have not entertained. Surely there must be some friends of his he would care to invite for dinner one evening? Charles replied that all his friends were away, at present, in the country, but that he would invite them next month upon their return. It is certainly strange that no one ever calls upon us.

25 August
Have not been able to write for several days due to the return of my illness — suffered acute pains and was violently sick again. Charles said he would move into the spare bedroom, so that I might obtain as much rest as possible. My darling is most attentive. Upon his return from the city in the evenings, he insists on making some soup or gruel and bringing it up to the bedroom, and then reads to me whilst I consume the liquid. I must confess however that I have little appetite.

1 September
What is wrong with me? I can hardly write these words, I am so weak. The medicine I take seems to do little good. I cannot eat any food, and when I manage to drink some soup I am only sick again. I have not been out of the house for nearly two weeks now. What is wrong with me? I am becoming such a burden to Charles. Would he have married

me if he had known that I would have become so ill?

4 September
No better. I feel so ill. Why is it that I am so ill? Why has God deprived me of my happiness?

5 September
I feel the end is coming. Why does Charles insist that I drink the soup when I am so unwell?

7 September
God help me. Charles has poisoned me. There is no escape.

'That is the last entry, sir,' said the constable closing the diary.

'Oh my God!' exclaimed Quinton burying his face in his hands.

'I believe your wife brought a sizeable inheritance to your marriage, sir, if I am not mistaken?' said Robertson leaning forwards and staring directly at his suspect.

'That is no concern of yours. I tell you I am innocent,' pleaded Quinton looking at the two policemen. 'Why don't you believe me?'

'That's as may be, sir. Constable, will you read the last entry again, if you please.'

'Yes sir — 'God help me. Charles has poisoned me. There is no escape',' replied the constable. 'The hand is very shaky, sir.'

''God help me. Charles has poisoned me. There is no escape',' repeated Robertson. 'Well Captain Quinton, I think that is all the proof we need. I would say that any jury in the land would convict you on that evidence. You will certainly hang, Captain Quinton — and very slowly if there is any justice in this world. Yes, you will hang very well indeed. Would you not agree, constable?'

'It would seem so, sir.'

'Take the prisoner away, and — oh Ravenscroft, see that this is all kept quiet for the time being.'

'Yes sir.'

1

Ledbury, September 1890

'What is this, my dear?' asked Ravenscroft looking over his spectacles at the bowl of thick, dark liquid which lay before him on the dinner table.

'Brown Windsor soup,' replied Lucy.

'I see.'

'You don't like it?'

'No . . . er . . . it's just that — '

'I can tell that you don't approve.'

'No, it's just that it is rather on the thick side,' said Ravenscroft submerging his spoon once again into the brown mixture.

'I think it is quite nice,' smiled Lucy after taking another mouthful.

'I expect that I shall probably grow to like it.'

'I think Susan has done rather well. I believe that it is a favourite of Queen Victoria.'

'Ah well, if it is good enough for Queen Victoria, then I am sure that it is certainly good enough for us,' smiled Ravenscroft before bringing the spoon to his mouth.

'There is no need for frivolity, Samuel. I

can tell you do not like it. It does have some of the Madeira in it,' said Lucy trying to sound enthusiastic.

'No, it's not the Madeira, it's just . . . well . . . just before we sat down I was reading the evening newspaper. It seems that a whole party of guests staying at one of the lodging houses in Pershore fell ill after eating a meal of Brown Windsor soup, pheasant pie and cheese.'

'Could it have been the pheasant pie?' suggested Lucy.

'Perhaps, but then it could have easily been the Brown Windsor soup. I suppose the dense, brown viscosity of the dish could hide anything of a suspicious nature.'

'I saw Susan prepare it — beef, lamb, vegetables, faggots of herbs.'

'Certainly a great deal of things.'

'Did any of these people die as a result of this meal?' asked Lucy becoming irritated by her husband's questioning.

'Yes, apparently one of the guests died during the night after eating the soup.'

'Well don't eat it if you don't want to. I'll ring for Susan to take it away,' said Lucy thrusting her spoon back into the bowl with a clatter

'No, don't do that. I'm sorry. I'm sure it is all right,' replied Ravenscroft taking another sip of the liquid. 'Actually it is quite pleasant.'

'I do wish you would make up your mind, Samuel.'

'I have. The soup is fine.'

'You are only saying that so as not to hurt my feelings.'

'No, not at all. It really is very good.'

'Now I come to think of it, it does have a rather peculiar odour,' said Lucy after taking another mouthful. 'I think we should leave it. Perhaps the lamb was not as fresh as it should have been. I will have a word with the butcher.'

'If you say so, but don't reject the dish on my account.'

'No, I don't like it. We should definitely leave it,' said Lucy ringing the small hand bell on the table.

'Now you are annoyed with me,' said Ravenscroft. 'I am sorry. I should not have mentioned it.'

'Ah, Susan, I think we have had enough of the Brown Windsor. If you would take it away please,' said Lucy ignoring her husband's last remark, and addressing the maid as she entered the room.

'Yes, ma'am,' replied the maid casting a suspicious eye at the half-full bowls.

Suddenly, the loud noise of the front doorbell being pressed broke the silence of the room.

'Surely that cannot be Tom Crabb again? It seems that every time we sit down to eat, our meal is interrupted by some police matter or other,' said an annoyed Lucy.

'Shall I tell him to wait, Mrs Ravenscroft, until after I have served the main course?' asked Susan.

'No, I suppose you had better let him in,' replied a resigned Lucy.

'I'm sorry, my dear. I am sure it must be something of great importance for Tom to call upon us at such a late hour,' suggested Ravenscroft hoping to placate his wife.

The maid left the room and returned a moment or two later. 'Please Mr Ravenscroft, it's not Constable Crabb. It's a young lad. Says he must speak to you most urgently.'

'Strange. Did this youth give his name?' asked Ravenscroft.

'No, sir,' replied the maid.

'Then I think you should instruct him to visit the police station. Tell him we are dining and cannot be disturbed,' instructed Lucy.

'Sorry to intrude, Mister Ravenscroft,' said a young man peering round the doorpost.

'Stebbins!' exclaimed Ravenscroft.

'Sorry for the interruption, Mister Ravenscroft, Mrs Ravenscroft,' said the smiling, fresh-faced youth removing his cap and stepping into the room. 'I knows you is dining, sir, but I thought you would want to know as soon as possible.'

'Who is this young man?' asked a bewildered Lucy.

'This is Stebbins, the boots whom I first encountered at the Tudor when I first visited Malvern,' explained Ravenscroft. 'What is it, Stebbins? You can see that we are busy at the moment?'

'Terrible business, sir. Poisoned he was!' pronounced the youth with a flourish.

'Who has been poisoned?' asked Ravenscroft regretting that he had asked the question, even before he had uttered the words.

'Him that ate the Brown Windsor, only he didn't. Him at Pershore. Maisie said he didn't eat it.'

'Stebbins, you are not making any sense. Wait in the kitchen until after we have finished our meal. Have you eaten?'

'No sir. Came as soon as I heard the news.'

'Then, Susan, you had better give him some food,' instructed Ravenscroft. 'May I suggest some of the Brown Windsor?'

'Thank you, Mister Ravenscroft. Don't like the look of that soup, though, if you don't mind my saying so,' replied Stebbins casting a glance at the half-empty bowls and turning up his nose. 'Looks a bit murky to me.'

'Here, young man, you mind what you are

saying,' reprimanded the maid.

'Take him to the kitchen, Susan,' repeated Ravenscroft.

The lad followed the maid out of the room.

'What a strange looking young man,' said Lucy after the door had been closed.

'He has rather a vivid imagination I'm afraid. Still he was helpful to us at Tewkesbury earlier this year.'

'How old is he?'

'Oh, about thirteen or fourteen I believe.'

'And you say you first met him at the Tudor in Malvern?' asked Lucy.

'Yes, he looked after me there. He was quite useful in providing me with food late at night, when the so called 'cure' prevented any indulgencies.'

'Sounds as though you had better see what he wants after dinner.'

* * *

'Now then, Stebbins, what is all this about?' asked Ravenscroft striding into the kitchen some minutes later.

'It's that gent in Pershore. Him that drank the soup, only he didn't, if you see what I means,' said Stebbins looking up from the table, his mouth full of bread and cheese.

'I take it you are referring to the party who

27

suffered ill effects from consuming the Brown Windsor soup?'

'Yes sir, they all had the soup and were ill, but the gent didn't, and he was the one that died,' announced Stebbins.

'I think you had better start at the beginning,' said Ravenscroft sighing as he sat down on one of the chairs. 'I did not know that you were living in Pershore. I thought you were still employed at the Hop Pole in Tewkesbury?'

'So I am sir.'

'Then how do you know what is going on in Pershore?'

'Ah well, Mister Ravenscroft. It's all on account of Maisie. She knows,' replied the youth tapping the side of his nose before cutting himself another large chunk of cheese and cramming it into his mouth.

'And who is this Maisie?' asked Ravenscroft wondering where all this line of inquiry was going.

'Maisie is my girl. She works at Talbots' Lodging House. Scullery maid she is. She saw everything.'

'Go on.'

'Well Maisie says that all the guests sat down that night to eat the Brown Windsor, and that they was all bad afterwards. Some of 'em worse than others. Only the gent that died, he didn't have any of the soup, but he was dead in his bed the next morning. Dead as a cold cucumber he was. All stiff and white he were. Been frothing at the mouth, his face all twisted in agony,' said Stebbins warming to his subject.

'Yes, yes, spare us the graphic details, Stebbins.'

'Well he were dead, as I said, Mister Ravenscroft. Dead!'

'And you say that the guest who died did not partake of the soup? Was the scullery maid sure on this point?' inquired Ravenscroft becoming more interested in the lad's account.

'My Maisie, she's a sharp one. She don't miss anything. If she says that gent didn't eat the Brown Windsor then he didn't,' said Stebbins springing to the maid's defence.

'It could have been the pheasant pie?' suggested Ravenscroft.

'Don't understand you, sir.'

'Well it could have been the pie, and not the soup, that was the cause of the guests all being ill, and perhaps the deceased gentleman ate rather more of it than the others? Do you know if this gentleman ate any of the pie?'

'Don't know,' muttered Stebbins looking deflated.

'Well there you are then,' said Ravenscroft

rising from the table.

'My Maisie, she had some of the pie,' said Stebbins hopefully.

'And was she ill?'

'No. So you sees, Mister Ravenscroft, it wasn't the pie at all. Nor was it the soup.'

'Did the scullery maid, this Maisie, did she eat some of the Brown Windsor — and was she ill afterwards?'

'No sir, she didn't have any of the soup,' said Stebbins helping himself to the last piece of cheese.

'So it must have been the soup, and not the pie that made all the people ill.'

'Yes Mister Ravenscroft, so you see that the gent must have been poisoned! One of them folks must have poisoned him! You has to do something about it,' pronounced Stebbins.

'Look, Stebbins, we don't know that anyone was poisoned. We do know that everyone who ate the soup was ill afterwards, but that they all recovered, and that the only person who died was the person who did not partake of the soup.'

'Exactly! So someone must have killed 'im off!'

'The gentleman who died could have been taking some kind of medicine for a particular ailment, and for one reason or another he accidentally took rather too much of it before

30

he retired. People are sometimes very careless with their medicines and how they use them. So you see there may be a perfectly fair explanation for all of this. You and this Maisie, Stebbins, must not go around telling everyone that the deceased was poisoned on purpose, when there is no evidence to suggest that this was the case,' said Ravenscroft seeking to curb the youth's enthusiasm.

'You wouldn't say that, Mister Ravenscroft, if you had seen 'im the morning after.'

'Did you?'

'No — but my Maisie did. It were 'er that found 'im.'

'Tell me what happened the next morning, after the maid found the deceased?'

'Well Maisie, she told Mister Talbot that gent was dead. Then they called the doctor.'

'And what did the doctor say?'

'Said he had eaten too much of the soup.'

'And then?'

'They took him away, to the undertakers.'

'I take it that the deceased man was all alone. There was no one who had accompanied him to the lodging house?' asked Ravenscroft.

'Not as far as I knows,'

'And how long had this gentleman been staying at the establishment?'

'Maisie says, about a week or so. What's

that got to do with it?'

'Well if this gentleman was hardly known to any of the other guests, why would any one of them have wanted to have poisoned him? No, it does not make any sense, Stebbins. What do the local police make of it?'

'Policeman who came after the doctor, asked a few questions, took away some of the soup, and that were it.'

'So the police have no reasons to investigate further?'

'Ah, but they don't know what you and I and Maisie knows, that the gent didn't eat any of the soup.'

'Then why on earth did Maisie not speak up when the policeman was there?' asked Ravenscroft.

'She couldn't do that.'

'Why ever not?'

'Cause she was out when the peeler came. She were getting the vituals for the evening meal.'

'So why didn't anyone else in the lodging house inform the policeman that the deceased had not eaten the soup?' sighed Ravenscroft.

'I don't know, does I? I weren't there at the time.'

'Look, Stebbins, I think that this is all rather fanciful.'

'No, sir. They killed him. You has to do

something about it Mister Ravenscroft. They be burying him tomorrow afternoon. Be too late then. You has to do something. You can't let them get away with it!' implored Stebbins jumping up from the chair and looking Ravenscroft directly in the face.

'Stebbins, please don't tell me what I can and cannot do,' replied Ravenscroft firmly as he turned away and opened the door for the youth.

'You 'as to do something. Please, Mister Ravenscroft. My Maisie is straight as a ruler. If she says something, it must be right. He were poisoned!' entreated the youth.

'All right, Stebbins, I think you have said enough for now. I'll think about it overnight. If there is nothing else on in the morning, then Constable Crabb and I will travel over to Pershore and make inquiries.'

'Lord bless you, sir! You won't regret it, Mister Ravenscroft.'

'Now, good night, Stebbins,' said Ravenscroft walking towards the front door and gesturing that Stebbins should leave.

'You mark my words, Mister Ravenscroft, he were done in, was that gent, and one of them folks in that place did it.'

'Good night, Stebbins,' said Ravenscroft opening the front door and indicating that the youth should step outside.

'Nice juicy case this one will be, I'll have no doubt, and remember it were Stebbins that told yer about it in the first place. You call on Stebbins if you need anything, Mister Ravenscroft. Stebbins is yer man.'

'Yes, good night, Stebbins,' sighed Ravenscroft closing the door on his uninvited guest.

2

Pershore

'Of course all this could be a complete waste of time, Tom. You realize that.'

'The lad's been right in the past, sir.'

'It all seems a bit too fanciful for me. However, it's a fine day, no crimes committed overnight, and we have nothing else to occupy our minds at the present, so it will do no harm to make inquiries,' added Ravenscroft as the trap made its way along the country lanes that led from Ledbury towards the county town of Pershore.

'So Stebbins never saw the body then?' asked Constable Crabb as he encouraged the horse to quicken his pace.

'No. It is all rather second-hand evidence, passed on by the scullery maid to Stebbins, and no doubt embellished by him. We shall probably discover that the dead man died from eating the Brown Windsor soup after all, and that there is nothing for us to investigate,' said Ravenscroft.

'Funny thing, soup. You never know what's in it, 'specially the cloudy ones.'

35

Ravenscroft smiled as the trap crossed the Severn at Upton.

★ ★ ★

An hour later the horse and trap made its way through the busy market place with its stalls and groups of people, and along the main street of the town lined with its elegant Georgian buildings and coaching inns, until Crabb pulled up the horse outside a drab looking building at the end of the road.

'Let us go and see what the local men have found out,' said Ravenscroft alighting from the trap and pushing open the door of the police station.

'No one about,' remarked Crabb following on behind and looking around the empty office.

Ravenscroft called out, and upon receiving no reply, the two men entered the smaller inner room.

'No wonder the office was unattended,' said Ravenscroft looking down at the armchair where a stocky, ruddy-faced, uniformed figure lay snoring loudly.

'Must have had a late night, sir,' smiled Crabb.

'Confound the fellow. Wake up, man!' shouted Ravenscroft.

The figure merely made a grunting sound

before continuing with his deep snores.

'This is intolerable!' exclaimed Ravenscroft leaning forwards and pushing the man's shoulder with a violent shove.

'Eh . . . what . . . the deuce . . . ' stuttered the uniformed officer.

'Wake up, man. Pull yourself together!' instructed Ravenscroft.

'What? Oh sorry, sir,' replied the man springing to his feet. 'I'm sorry, sir. You must forgive me. How can I help you, sir?'

'Don't you know that such conduct is a gross dereliction of duty?' reprimanded Ravenscroft.

'Sorry, sir. And you are?'

'Ravenscroft. You have heard of me? Detective Inspector Ravenscroft.'

'Oh my God!' exclaimed the embarrassed policeman growing even redder in the face as he quickly brushed down his tunic with his hands and attempted to straighten out his collar. 'I'm sorry, sir. Please excuse me. I don't know what came over me.'

'You know you can be sacked for this,' joined in Crabb.

'Yes, I'm sorry, sir. It will not happen again I can assure you. This has never happened before. You must — '

'Stop babbling on, man,' said an annoyed Ravenscroft.

'Yes, sir. Sorry, sir.'

'Who are you?'

'Hoskings, sir. P.C. Hoskings,' replied the policeman shuffling his feet and growing even redder in the face.

'Well, Hoskings, where is Sergeant Braithwaite?'

'Away, sir.'

'Away?'

'Ill, sir. Laid up with a broken leg in Worcester Infirmary, sir.'

'I see. So you are in charge?'

'Yes sir. Until they can find a replacement.'

'Well Hoskings, I suppose you will have to do. Now what can you tell Constable Crabb and myself about this poisoning case?' asked Ravenscroft.

'Poisoning case? Oh yes, sir. Nasty case of food poisoning at Talbots' Lodging House. Everyone ate the soup and was ill afterwards. Brown Windsor I believe. Only one gent ate too much and died as a result. Wonder they didn't all die.'

'And you went to investigate?'

'Yes sir.'

'Well, what happened, man?'

'Doctor Homer was already there when I arrived. The man was lying on his bed. He was quite dead. Seemed he had eaten too much of the soup.'

38

'Only he hadn't,' interjected Crabb.

'Go on,' urged Ravenscroft.

'Well, I . . . er . . . interviewed Mr Talbot, that's the owner of the lodging house, who confirmed that they had all been ill through drinking the soup, then we called in Johnsons' the undertakers and they took the deceased away. That was all there was to it, sir.'

'I believe there was probably a lot more to it, Hoskings. That is what we have come to find out. Did you interview any of the other members of the party?'

'No, sir. Didn't see the need to, sir. Seemed a straightforward case.'

'That will be for us to judge.'

'Yes, sir. Of course, sir.'

'We understand that you took a sample of the soup away with you?' asked Ravenscroft.

'Er . . . well sir . . . I . . . er.'

'For goodness sake, man, did you, or did you not, take away a sample of the soup for further investigation?' asked Ravenscroft becoming annoyed.

'Yes sir,' replied Hoskings looking sheepishly down at his boots.

'Well, man, where is it then?'

'I'm afraid there was an accident, sir.'

'Accident? What do you mean an accident? Speak up, man.'

'Sorry, sir. I was carrying the jar back to the police station when it slipped out of my hand and fell to the ground. I'm afraid there is none of the soup left. I'm very sorry, sir. I couldn't help it, sir.'

'Good gracious, man!' exclaimed Ravenscroft. 'That could have been valuable evidence.'

'I'm sorry, sir.'

'Your carelessness may have profound consequences for the investigation of this case.'

'Yes, sir. Sorry, sir.'

'And stop saying you're sorry all the time,' said Ravenscroft, glaring.

'No, sir. Sorry, sir, I mean yes, sir.'

'All right. Now we understand that the man is due to be buried this afternoon. I presume the body is still at the undertakers. You best come with us and show us the way.'

'I'm sorry, sir. The deceased was buried this morning.'

'What do you mean, he was buried this morning? It has only just gone twelve,' said Ravenscroft feeling more and more frustrated.

'Buried earlier this morning, sir. About two hours ago, I believe,' muttered the crestfallen policeman.

'For goodness sake!' exclaimed Ravenscroft.

40

'If we had known this, Tom, we would have come earlier. Confound it!'

'We will have to get an exhumation order, sir,' offered Crabb.

'On what grounds, Tom? We don't even know if someone deliberately poisoned the man, or whether it was the soup after all that killed him. We will never be able to obtain an order. So now we have no corpse, and now that Police Constable Hoskings here has destroyed all the evidence, we have nothing to go on at all!' said a dispirited Ravenscroft.

'I'm sorry, sir.'

'Look Hoskings, when you entered the dead man's bedroom, did you notice anything unusual there?'

'Unusual, sir?' asked the perplexed constable.

'Yes, Hoskings. Were there any signs that a struggle had taken place?'

'No, sir.'

'Did you observe any bottles or other medicine on the bedside cabinet for instance?'

'I don't think so, sir. I didn't really notice . . . ' trailed off Hoskings.

'For goodness sake. Come, Crabb, I can see that we are wasting our time here. We shall have to go and visit this Talbots' Lodging House for ourselves and see if we can arrive at the truth of the matter.'

'What would you like me to do, sir?' asked Hoskings.

'Nothing, Hoskings. You had better remain here. I think you have done more than enough as far as this case is concerned.'

'Yes, sir. Sorry, sir.'

'If you want something to do, you can clean up this room. It looks a mess, man. Then you can tidy yourself up as well,' said Ravenscroft beginning to leave.

'Yes, sir.'

'And Hoskings — '

'Yes, sir?'

'Try not to fall asleep again.'

'No, sir.'

★   ★   ★

A few minutes later Ravenscroft and Crabb made their way up the road that took them away from the centre of the town and onwards towards a large, shabby, four-storeyed, half-timbered building situated at the end of a driveway where they found a faded and chipped sign bearing the words *TALBOTS*' in large letters swinging somewhat precariously over the front door.

Ravenscroft grasped the large bellpull and was rewarded by the sound of ringing somewhere in the distance.

'Looks as though the place has seen better days,' said Crabb glancing apprehensively at the sign above their heads.

'Good morning, sir,' said a young red-headed, sallow-faced girl opening the door.

'Good morning,' replied Ravenscroft removing his hat. 'I wonder if I might have a word with your master, Mr Talbot?'

'Yes, sir. If you would care to wait a moment, sir, I will go and get him for you,' said the maid disappearing down what appeared to be a long hallway.

'I wonder if she is Stebbin's girl, Maisie?' whispered Crabb.

A few moments later a small, thin, shabbily dressed man made his way along the hallway towards the policemen. 'Good morning, sir. I expect you have come to see the room. It will be ready shortly, and at only six shillings a week including all meals, and a change of linen on Mondays. You will find nothing better in Pershore, I can assure you.'

'No Mr Talbot, we have not come about the room. My name is Detective Inspector Ravenscroft, and this is my colleague Constable Crabb.'

'I see. Forgive me, I had not observed your constable's attire.'

'Who is it, Talbot?' boomed a loud voice from somewhere at the far end of the hallway.

43

'It is the police, my dear,' replied the lodging-house owner forcing a brief smile through clenched teeth.

'Tell them to go away, Talbot. Room ain't available yet. Tell them someone has already been and made enquiries,' continued the voice.

'I know that Constable Hoskings has called upon you already, but the matter has now reached a more senior level,' said Ravenscroft.

'What's that?' shouted the voice.

'Gent says he needs to make further enquiries. Something about a more senior level — ' began Talbot.

'What senior level?' asked the owner of the voice suddenly emerging from the interior of the building and striding towards the front door.

'Good morning. I take it I have the honour of addressing Mrs Talbot?' said Ravenscroft somewhat taken aback by the large, red-faced, buxom woman who seemed now to occupy the whole width of the front doorway and who stared at him, in what he considered to be an unfriendly manner.

'Talbot and I have told everything there is to tell — and that's an end to it. Close the door, Talbot,' instructed the woman casting a dismissive glance at Ravenscroft before turning upon her heel.

44

'I am sorry, but Mrs Talbot has spoken,' said the small man in a nervous way as he began to close the door on the two policemen.

'I am afraid that I must insist on speaking to you both,' said Ravenscroft placing his foot in the doorway. 'I can of course return with a warrant. There have been certain irregularities.'

'Irregularities!' said Mrs Talbot quickly returning to the scene. 'Irregularities? What irregularities? I'll have you know that Talbot and I run a very respectable establishment here. You'll find none of your irregularities here.'

'I'm sure not, Mrs Talbot. Your establishment comes very highly recommended,' replied Ravenscroft seeking to placate the formidable woman.

'Highly recommended? Who says so?' asked Mrs Talbot.

'Er . . . the Duke of Welshpool,' stammered Ravenscroft.

'Did you hear that, Mrs Talbot. The Duke of Welshpool no less,' said the lodging-house owner.

'He was most complimentary,' added Ravenscroft attempting to smile.

'Don't remember no Duke of Welshpool staying here,' said the woman in a more conciliatory tone.

'I believe it was a few years ago, before he

inherited the title,' continued Ravenscroft anxious to obtain access to the building.

'Highly recommended you say?'

'Yes indeed, ma'am. The best lodging house for miles, he said. He particularly praised the cooking,' continued Ravenscroft realizing that he was now slowly gaining the advantage.

'Did you hear that, my dear. I have always said your cooking could not be bettered, and that it would bring us fame and fortune one day,' said Talbot.

'We just wanted to ask you a few questions concerning your late guest,' said Ravenscroft easing himself slowly into the hall. 'The constable who visited you failed to carry out the correct procedures. The fault is not on your part, I can assure you. We have been asked to clarify one or two points. I am sure we will not detain you for more than a few minutes or so.'

The landlady stared hard at Ravenscroft.

'It can do no harm, my dear,' said Talbot.

'Very well then. You better come into the dining room,' sighed his wife.

'Thank you,' replied Ravenscroft as he and Crabb followed the couple down the long corridor and into a large room.

'You best take a seat,' instructed Mrs Talbot indicating one of the chairs gathered round a large mahogany table.

'Thank you. What a pleasant room,' lied Ravenscroft glancing around at the simple furniture and drab wallpaper, before looking up at the large faded print, depicting a battle scene, that hung above the fireplace.

'Inkerman,' pronounced Mrs Talbot observing Ravenscroft's interest. 'Tell them, Talbot, you was there.'

'You were at Inkerman?' asked Ravenscroft.

'Go on tell them,' instructed the landlady.

'I am sure that the inspector has not come here today to talk about the war, my dear. How can we help you?' asked Talbot, hastily changing the subject.

'I wonder if you could tell us something about your late guest, Mr Talbot?' asked Ravenscroft.

'Very little I'm afraid, inspector. Mr Jones was not with us very long. He arrived just over a week ago. He was not a man of many words. He kept very much to himself,' replied Talbot.

'Can you describe him for us?' asked Ravenscroft. 'Unfortunately Mr Jones was buried before we could inspect the body.'

'Well I suppose he was quite ordinary really, probably forty years of age I would say — '

'More like fifty, Talbot,' interrupted Mrs Talbot.

'Fairly stout in build,' continued the lodging-house keeper.

'Rather thin.'

'Fairly reddish, with a fresh-faced complexion.'

'Very grey-looking surely, Talbot.'

'Did this Mr Jones come alone to your establishment?' interrupted Ravenscroft realizing that the couple would never agree in their description of their former lodger.

'Yes, he came alone,' said Talbot.

'How long did he intend staying?'

'I don't understand.'

'When he arrived did the gentleman tell you how long he intended staying with you?'

'He said he would probably stay for two or three weeks; he could not be sure,' replied Talbot.

'There was something rather strange about him now I come to think of it,' said Mrs Talbot.

'Yes, go on,' encouraged Ravenscroft.

'He did not appear to have much luggage with him. No trunks or large cases, only a small bag not much bigger than a Gladstone. I remember remarking to Talbot that it seemed a bit strange at the time.'

'I see. Do you still have this bag, or any of the deceased's possessions?' asked Ravenscroft hopefully.

48

'Burnt them all, didn't we, Talbot?' remarked the woman.

'I see,' said a disappointed Ravenscroft. 'I wonder if you could describe the contents of the bag?'

'Nothing much, mainly old clothes, a bible and such like.'

'Was there anything of a personal nature — letters, papers, a diary perhaps?'

'No, I don't think so,' replied Talbot looking up at his wife.

'An engraved pocket watch or knife?'

'No, there was nothing of that nature,' said Mrs Talbot starting to busy herself in laying out the cutlery on the table.

'Strange,' said Ravenscroft. 'I wonder if you would be so kind as to describe the events of the evening, before everyone fell ill? I understand you ate a meal of Brown Windsor soup, pheasant pie and cheese. Is that correct?'

'Yes. They said it were the Brown Windsor that made everyone ill, but it weren't my fault, and it's no use you suggesting otherwise,' said Mrs Talbot resuming her defensive manner once more.

'Nothing wrong with Mrs Talbot's cooking,' said Talbot springing to the defence of his wife.

'It were that meat. We always have the best cuts for our guests, but that silly girl Maisie, she went to the butchers who sold her that old meat. I thought it looked a bit strange at the time, and before I could do anything about it she had mixed it all up with everything else in the pot,' continued the landlady looking away sheepishly.

'And did everyone partake of this soup?' asked Ravenscroft leaning forwards.

'Yes, I believe so,'

'Even the deceased gentleman?'

'Yes,' replied a hesitant Talbot.

'Mrs Talbot?' asked Ravenscroft addressing the woman.

'Yes, but it weren't my fault if he ate too much. We was not to know that he would go and die on us like that,' said Mrs Talbot. 'We was not to know that he had a dicky constitution, were we?'

'No, of course not. Tell me, were all your guests present at this meal?' asked Ravenscroft.

'Yes.'

'And what happened when you had all dined?'

'They all went back to their respective rooms,' answered Talbot.

'And when did you begin to feel unwell?'

'Two or three hours afterwards. It weren't till the morning of course that we found that all the others had been unwell as well.'

'Could you tell us the names of your guests, and how long they have been with you?' asked Ravenscroft. 'Crabb, make a note if you please.'

'Yes, sir,' said Crabb removing his pocket-book and pencil from the top pocket of his tunic.

'Well. There is the old Jewish Professor, Jacobson, he is in number one, with his wife. They have been with us for nearly five years now. Strange couple: he must be three times the age she is. Then there is that nice gentleman Mr Cherrington in number five. He has only been here for the past three weeks: a perfect gentleman, quietly spoken, no trouble at all. Count Turco, he is a musician from Italy, bit excitable like all them foreigners, always playing that violin of his, but such beautiful melodies, I could listen to them all day I could,' said Mrs Talbot relishing the opportunity to tell Ravenscroft all that she knew. 'Then there are the Misses Fanshaw in number four, two respectable ladies in their seventies who have been with us for over ten years. In number three there is Mr Claybourne. He is what you call a commercial gentlemen. He spends only two or three days with us every week during his travels. I believe he lives mainly in London. That is all I should think.'

'You have forgotten Miss Martin,' said Talbot hesitantly.

'Ah yes, we should not forget Miss Martin. Would that we could. Would that we could, Talbot. I'm sure that you would like to if you had half a chance,' said the woman rising to her full height and giving her husband a disapproving look.

'Now then, Letita my dear, that is all in the past,' said Talbot looking down uneasily at the floor.

'And is there anyone else who resides in the house, who was there that night?' asked Ravenscroft.

'Only Maisie, the housemaid. You saw her when you came in,' replied Mrs Talbot continuing with her table laying.

'And you say that everyone ate the soup, and that you were all ill afterwards?' asked Crabb looking up from his pocketbook.

'That's what we said, young man. Why don't you listen? Why do you have to keep going on about it,' snapped the landlady.

'Well thank you, Mrs Talbot. We may need to question your guests later. We won't take up anymore of your time. We can see you are busy,' said Ravenscroft standing up. 'Oh, one more thing just before we go. I wonder if we might see the room where the late gentleman resided.'

'What you want to do that for?' asked Mrs Talbot.

'It may be of assistance to us.'

'We ain't cleaned it yet,' protested Talbot.

'That is of no consequence, but I can see you are both busy people, so perhaps your housemaid could accompany us there,' suggested Ravenscroft.

'Suppose it won't matter. Maisie! Maisie!' shouted Mrs Talbot. 'Where is that idle silly girl?'

'Sorry Mrs Talbot,' said the maid rushing into the room holding a cleaning cloth.

'Maisie, show these gentlemen Mr Jones's old room,' instructed the landlady.

'Yes, ma'am,' said the maid. 'If you would care to follow me, gentlemen.'

Ravenscroft and Crabb followed the girl up two flights of a narrow creaking staircase, until they reached a small landing with two doors facing each other.

'In here, gentlemen,' indicated the maid opening one of the two doors.

'Thank you. Who occupies the room opposite?' asked Ravenscroft as he and Crabb entered the bedroom.

'Miss Martin, sir.'

'I see. Come in, Maisie, and close the door behind you if you will.'

'Yes, sir,' replied the girl complying with Ravenscroft's request.

'Now then Maisie, you know why we are here?'

''Cus Stebbins told you what I said.'

'And what exactly was that Maisie?' asked Ravenscroft giving the girl an encouraging smile in an attempt to put her at her ease.

'That the gentleman did not eat the soup, sir,' said the girl looking down nervously at her feet.

'Are you sure Mr Jones did not consume any of the soup? Both Mr and Mrs Talbot have led us to believe that he did.'

'Yes, sir. Gent didn't eat any of it. I served out the soup for everyone, but when I collected up the bowls I noticed that his was still full. He hadn't taken so much as a spoonful.'

'Oh, why was that?'

'Don't know. Perhaps he didn't like to taste the Windsor. He was very quiet like. Didn't say much. Seemed miles away,' continued the maid.

'I see. That is interesting.'

'Didn't eat much at all.'

'And what happened after the meal?'

'They all went back to their rooms.'

'We understand that it was you who found the deceased?'

'Yes, sir. When the gent didn't come down for breakfast, master sent me up to knock on his door and see if he was all right, especially as we had all been ill in the night.'

54

'And what happened next?' asked Ravenscroft encouragingly.

'Well it were all quiet, sir, so I opened the door, and that's when I found him. He were dead, sir. Lying on the bed. It were horrible. Horrible. Can I go now, sir? I don't know anything else,' replied the maid anxiously turning to leave the room.

'One more thing, Maisie, just before you go,' said Ravenscroft. 'Who cleared out the dead man's possessions?'

'Mr Talbot. sir, after they had taken the body away.'

'Thank you, Maisie, you may go. Constable Crabb and I will make our own way out in a few minutes.'

'Did I do right, sir, in telling Stebbins?' asked the maid looking anxiously at Ravenscroft.

'You did absolutely right, Maisie. Thank you.'

The maid curtsied and left the room closing the door behind her.

'Well, Tom, what do you make of all this?' asked Ravenscroft.

'Looks as though he didn't have the soup after all.'

'Yes, she was quite clear on that point, despite what the Talbots said. So I think we can assume that it was not the soup that caused the poor man to die. If only we had got here yesterday we could have seen the body. Now we have no way of telling whether he died from poisoning, or from natural causes. If he was poisoned, then we have to ask ourselves, how — and why.'

'Can't see why the Talbots would have had any cause to kill him,' suggested Crabb.

'No, I cannot see any reason either. In fact why would any of them in this house have wanted to poison him? The man had only been here for just over a week. Nevertheless, I think the Talbots are hiding something from us. I don't believe they destroyed all the dead man's possessions, as they claim they did. Then there is all that nonsense about Talbot being at Inkerman in the Crimean War. He might be of the right age, but a man of his stature and character would have been of little use to the British army. Let's have a look round this miserable room.'

'Just a bed, table and chairs,' said Crabb. 'Pretty drab sort of place if you ask me.'

'Nothing of a personal nature at all. Partial view of the garden through the window. Otherwise there is nothing left to suggest that it was occupied by anyone at all. Have a look under the bed, Tom. Something may have dropped on the floor.'

Crabb got down on his knees and stared

56

into the darkened space beneath the mattress. 'Can't see anything here, sir. No, yes, what is that? Small piece of paper, sir.'

'Let me see, Tom.'

Crabb handed the small fragment to Ravenscroft.

'*S. WORCESTER. SEPTEMBER 12.3 p.m.*' read Ravenscroft. 'Looks as though it has been torn from part of a letter. I wonder what that means? Place and time probably. Could be referring to a meeting of some kind.'

'Might have been there for years, sir. Could have come from some other guest,' suggested Crabb.

'You're probably right, Tom. Still I'll keep it just in case,' said Ravenscroft folding up the paper and placing it inside his wallet.

'What now, sir?'

'I think we should visit this Doctor Homer. He examined the deceased man, so perhaps he can throw some light on this affair.'

★ ★ ★

'I don't really see how I can help you, inspector,' said the grey-haired general practitioner. 'It was perfectly clear to me that the man had died from eating the Brown Windsor soup. I believe that everyone in the

57

house had also been ill.'

It was a few minutes later and Ravenscroft and Crabb were standing in the dimly lit surgery of Doctor Homer, which was situated in a Georgian house lower down the main street of the town.

'But they did not die,' said Ravenscroft.

'No, but the poor man must have eaten more than the others. Then again perhaps his constitution was not as it should have been.'

'Forgive me, doctor, but did you not think it prudent to refer this man's death to the local coroner?'

'No.'

'May I ask why not?' asked Ravenscroft.

'Simply because I could not see that there was any foul play involved. As I have just said, everyone in the house had apparently also been ill from drinking the soup and this man must have eaten more than the others,' replied Homer showing signs of annoyance.

'I see.'

'Now if you will excuse me, I am already late for my rounds,' replied the doctor picking up a black bag that had lain on the desk.

'Just one more question, Doctor Homer — did you notice any bottles or any other kinds of medication in the bedroom?'

'No. There was nothing on the bedside table, not even a glass. Will that be all?'

'Yes, thank you for your time. We will not detain you.'

* * *

Ravenscroft and Crabb made their way back up the main street of the town towards the waiting trap.

'Well, Tom, it would seem that we have been wasting our time after all. In view of the fact that we don't even have a body to examine, and as we have conflicting evidence as to whether the deceased did, or did not, consume the soup on the night in question, I don't see how we can proceed any further. In addition to all that, we have no personal items remaining to tell us more about the said gentleman, nor can we find out whether he was poisoned or just died of natural causes. Then there doesn't seem to be any reason why anyone would have wanted to have killed him. He had only recently arrived here, and was alone, and apparently kept very much to himself.'

'I'm inclined to agree with you, sir,' said Crabb.

'Then let us return to Ledbury. No body, no personal possessions, no evidence, no motive. There just doesn't seem to be any kind of case for us to investigate. None at all.'

3

Ledbury and Pershore

'I'm afraid it was a complete waste of time, our journey to Pershore yesterday,' said Ravenscroft tapping the top of his egg with his spoon.

'So you keep saying, Samuel,' remarked Lucy.

'I'm sorry. I was not aware that I had mentioned it this morning — but then I expect you are right. It must be because I have nothing to interest me at the present. I think all the criminals have left town for the fruit picking on the nearby farms.'

'Would that we could leave as well,' sighed Lucy. 'It seems ages since we went on holiday. I think the children might enjoy a few days at the seaside.'

'Anywhere in particular?' asked Ravenscroft trying not to sound too enthusiastic.

'I hear that Weymouth is very pleasant at this time of the year.'

'And what are the attractions of that particular place?'

'I believe it is quite fashionable. It has a

splendid promenade and harbour, and the beaches are quite extensive. I think we could both do with a change, and the children would so enjoy it, I know,' said Lucy optimistically.

'I see that you have been fruitful in your research, my dear. I suppose I might be able to arrange a few days away from this den of criminality.'

'Oh Samuel, how splendid!' exclaimed Lucy.

'I am due some leave, and as I said there is nothing much happening in the town at this time of the year. I'll have a word with the Superintendent and see if we could go next week for a few days. I'm sure Tom would be able to keep an eye on things,' replied Ravenscroft warming to the idea.

'I shall need a new dress.'

'Of course, new dresses are always required for excursions to the seaside.'

'Ah, Susan, you have brought us the post,' said Lucy acknowledging the entrance of the maid.

'Just the three this morning, ma'am,' said Susan placing the silver salver on the table.

'It is to be hoped that they are not accounts to be settled. I do not think I could face another demand at the present when there is a new dress to be purchased,' teased

Ravenscroft as he dissected his egg with a spoon.

'This one must be for you, Samuel,' said Lucy passing over a small blue envelope to her husband.

'Interesting. I don't believe I recognize the hand. It just says 'Ravenscroft. Ledbury.' Quite poorly written with an unsteady hand. Posted yesterday,' said Ravenscroft examining the outside of the envelope.

'Why don't you just open it and see,' instructed Lucy.

Ravenscroft reached for the letter opener. 'Perhaps it is that strange aunt of yours. The one you keep telling me about, who is always threatening to come and visit us. Aunt Alice, or Agnes, or whatever her name is. Then again it could be from an admirer.'

'You don't have any admirers,' interjected Lucy.

'One must live in expectation. Perhaps we should leave it until the evening,' said Ravenscroft laying down the envelope before taking a mouthful of egg.

'Well if you won't open it, I will,' said Lucy reaching out across the table.

'No, I think I shall open it after all,' said Ravenscroft swiftly picking up the envelope and opening the flap with the opener. 'Quite extraordinary!' he exclaimed after a few moments reading its contents.

'Well, who is it from?' asked Lucy impatiently.

'I don't know. The letter is unsigned, on blue paper. It just says — *Jones was poisoned. It was the tawny.* That is all,' replied Ravenscroft passing over the letter to his wife.

'Jones was the name of the man who died from eating the Brown Windsor?'

'Yes, but the maid told Tom and me that he did not eat any of the soup — and this letter would tend to suggest that the poor man was poisoned by another means.'

'The tawny port?'

'Yes, but if this man did die from poison in his port, why did no one else die from drinking it?' asked a puzzled Ravenscroft.

'Perhaps he was the only one who liked port?' suggested Lucy.

'Yes, that could be the case I suppose. It looks as though Tom and I will have to go back to Pershore, and find out who wrote this letter, and see if we can recover that port before anyone else drinks it,' said Ravenscroft rising swiftly from the breakfast table.

'I suppose this could mean the end of our holiday,' sighed Lucy.

'Not at all, my dear. I am sure that we shall be able to clear all this up in a day or so. We'll go next Monday. Yes, Monday it shall be. I'll write to the Superintendent. Meanwhile, why don't you consult the Bradshaw in respect of our journey, and also see what suitable establishments there are in Weymouth.'

★   ★   ★

'Well, Tom, here we are again,' said Ravenscroft as he and Crabb walked up the path to Talbots' lodging house.

'Be interesting if we can find out who sent you that letter.'

'We must hope that no one else has drunk any of the tawny. Ah, I think that is Mr Talbot himself standing on the doorstep. Good day to you, Mr Talbot,' called out Ravenscroft.

'Lord save us,' muttered the landlord pulling a glum face. 'Whatever is Mrs Talbot going to say? She won't like this at all. Not at all.'

'I'm sorry to have to impose ourselves on you and your good wife once again, but I am afraid something serious has arisen regarding the late Mr Jones.'

'Who's that, Talbot?' shouted a familiar voice from within the dark interior of the building.

'It's that inspector again, my dear,' replied Talbot wiping a dirty hand across his stained red waistcoat.

'What!' exclaimed Mrs Talbot striding up to the doorway.

'Told you she would not like it,' mumbled Talbot.

'Good morning, Mrs Talbot,' said a smiling Ravenscroft ignoring the last remark. 'I trust I find you in good health.'

'What do you want? We told you everything yesterday,' grumbled the landlady adopting a defensive pose.

'Indeed you did, Mrs Talbot, and Constable Crabb and I were most grateful for your assistance, but something of great importance has arisen since then. We believe that you and your husband, and your guests, may be in the gravest danger.'

'Gravest danger?' asked the landlady.

'Indeed so, Mrs Talbot. Perhaps if my Constable and I could come inside we could explain everything, and then this matter can be quickly resolved,' said Ravenscroft realizing that perhaps he had only this one opportunity to gain re-admittance to the boarding house.

'Could be important, my dear,' said Talbot.

'Oh, very well. You best come in then.'

'Thank you,' said Ravenscroft giving a sideways glance at Crabb, before the two of them followed the couple down the hall and into the dining room.

'Well, get on with it then,' snapped the landlady. 'We haven't got all day. This is a busy establishment.'

'Can you tell me what your guests usually drink with their meals?' asked Ravenscroft looking quickly around the room.

'Why?' demanded Mrs Talbot.

'It is very important. In particular I would like to know what Mister Jones drank on the night in question?'

'Each of our guests has their own particular bottle,' said Talbot leading the way across the room to where a large collection of bottles stood together on an old wooden tray.

'And what did Mr Jones drink?' asked Ravenscroft anxious to know more.

'The tawny,' interjected Mrs Talbot. 'He were very fond of the tawny. Would let no one else drink it, he said. He were most particular.'

'And did Mr Jones partake of his usual drink on the night in question?'

'I suppose so.'

'When did he drink from the bottle?'

'What you mean — when did he drink?' asked Mrs Talbot.

'At the beginning of the meal, or at the conclusion?'

'He always finished off the meal with his usual glass of port,' offered Talbot.

'And did he do the same that night?'

'Yes, I believe so.'

'What happened after he had drunk the

port?' continued Ravenscroft.

'What do you mean, 'what happened'?'

'Did Mr Jones complain of feeling unwell?'

'No. He just got up from the table and went straight upstairs to his room, if I recall,' said the landlady.

'Can you tell me which of these bottles is the port?' asked Ravenscroft.

Talbot searched through the group. 'It ain't here. Bottle ain't here.'

'Are you sure?' asked an anxious Ravenscroft.

'I tells you it ain't here. Have a look for yourself if you don't believe me.'

Ravenscroft stepped forwards and carefully examined the bottles. 'I see that you write the name of each of your guests on the labels of the bottles.'

'Yes,' replied Talbot. 'That's so everyone knows their own bottle.'

'Have either you or your wife removed the bottle since Mister Jones's demise?' asked Ravenscroft.

'I ain't. Has you, my dear?' Talbot asked his wife.

'No, perhaps that girl has thrown it away. Maisie, Maisie,' called the landlady.

The maid quickly entered the room. 'Yes Mrs Talbot.'

'Have you gone and thrown Mister Jones's

bottle of tawny away?' enquired Talbot.

'No Mr Talbot,' replied the maid giving Ravenscroft a fleeting glance.

'Are you sure on that point, Maisie?' asked Ravenscroft.

'Yes sir. I have not taken it away.'

'What is all this about?' asked an irritated Mrs Talbot.

'We have reason to believe that the poison that killed your late guest was contained within the bottle of port,' replied Ravenscroft. 'Mister Jones did not die from eating too much of the Brown Windsor, or any other item of food, but through taking his usual glass of port.'

'Good heavens!' exclaimed the landlady.

'Lord help us!' echoed Talbot.

'Maisie, it is very important that we find this bottle. Do you think you could go and see if it has been included in any items of rubbish that may be in the vicinity,' instructed Ravenscroft.

'Yes sir,' said the maid quickly leaving the room.

'How do you know this port was poisoned, if we don't have the bottle?' asked Mrs Talbot.

'We have received certain information that suggests that is the case,' replied Ravenscroft.

'What you mean — certain information?' asked Talbot.

'I am not at liberty to reveal where this

information was obtained.'

'I knows where it came from, Talbot. It's that Miss Martin.'

'You don't know that at all,' sighed Talbot.

'Yes it will be her, I have no doubt. Our prim and pretty Miss Martin. Always anxious to spread rumour and innuendo about this establishment,' protested Mrs Talbot.

'Not that again,' muttered Talbot turning away.

'Please sir,' said the maid entering the room. 'I've looked where we keep the rubbish, but there is no bottle of tawny there.'

'Thank you, Maisie. So it would seem that whoever put poison in that bottle must have removed it shortly after Mr Jones drank some of the contents,' said Ravenscroft.

'Well it ain't any use your looking at either me or Mrs Talbot,' said the landlord. 'We had no reason to go round killing our guests.'

'And I had nothing to do with it,' added the maid.

'I am sure you did not. Nevertheless I believe that a serious crime has taken place in the household, and that investigations need to be carried out to discover the truth. I will need to question all your guests.'

'They are not all here at present,' said Talbot.

'Then we shall start now with the ones who

are,' said Ravenscroft adopting a more formal, serious tone.

'Shall I go and ask them to come down?' asked Crabb.

'No, thank you. I think we will interview your guests in their rooms.'

'What do you want us to do?' asked a bewildered Talbot.

'It will be quite in order for you both to go about your usual business,' said Ravenscroft. 'Perhaps you will allow your maid to show us the way.'

'Yes, yes, I suppose so.'

'Thank you. Maisie, will you lead on,' instructed Ravenscroft.

★ ★ ★

Ravenscroft and Crabb followed the maid onto the first-floor landing where three doors faced them.

'Which one would you like to see first, sir?'

'Can you tell us who resides here?' asked Ravenscroft, indicating the first door.

'That will be Professor Jacobson and his wife,' replied the maid.

'And there?'

'That's Mister Claybourne's room. He is away in London at present. And that is where Miss Fanshaw and her sister reside,' replied

70

the maid pointing to the third room.

'Then I think we will begin with Professor Jacobson. Will you be kind enough to announce us. But one thing before then — was it you who sent us this letter?' asked Ravenscroft removing the paper from his pocket.

'No sir. I didn't send you no letter.'

'You are sure on that point?' Ravenscroft looked intently into the maid's eyes.

'Yes, sir. I know nothing about any letter.'

'Thank you, Maisie. If you would kindly announce us.'

The maid tapped gently on the wood.

'Yes, Maisie,' said a woman's voice from the partially opened door.

'There is a gentleman here who would like a word with you and Professor Jacobson, ma'am,' said Maisie.

'Permit me. My name is Detective Inspector Ravenscroft, and this is my colleague, Constable Crabb. We are making inquiries regarding the sudden demise of Mr Jones,' said Ravenscroft. 'Thank you, Maisie, you may go now, I think we can find our own way around.'

The young woman paused momentarily, looking intently at Ravenscroft, before opening the door wider. 'You had better come in, gentlemen.'

'Who is it, Rosanna?' called out an older voice from within the room.

'Two gentlemen enquiring about poor Mr Jones,' said the young lady addressing an elderly grey-haired man with a long flowing beard who was seated in a leather armchair.

'Detective Inspector Ravenscroft and Constable Crabb,' repeated Ravenscroft entering the book-lined room.

'Forgive me, gentlemen, if I do not stand. Rosanna, please offer the gentlemen chairs. You say you have come about our late lodger. Talbot mentioned that you had visited him yesterday. How can we help you?' asked Jacobson staring out across the room.

'Thank you,' replied Ravenscroft accepting one of the chairs, as Crabb stood by the door. 'Can I ask whether you were both present at the evening meal on the night that Mr Jones died?'

'Yes,' replied the professor's wife walking across the room and positioning herself by the side of the old man's chair.

'Did either of you notice anything unusual occurring at the meal?'

'I am afraid I saw nothing, inspector. I lost my sight some years ago,' said Professor Jacobson.

'I am sorry,' apologized Ravenscroft.

'I am quite dependent on my wife now. She is my eyes. She takes good care of me. I want for nothing.'

Ravenscroft observed that the young woman with the black swept-backed hair and pale complexion looked down uneasily at her feet. 'Mrs Jacobson, did you notice anything unusual?'

'Er, no.'

'I believe everyone was ill after consuming the Brown Windsor?' asked Ravenscroft.

'Yes, unfortunately so, but we were well again by the morning,' replied Mrs Jacobson.

'The cooking leaves a lot to be desired in this establishment, but we manage to survive,' smiled Jacobson.

'Can you tell me anything about Mr Jones?'

'I do not understand you,' replied the old man bringing his thin wrinkled hands together and placing them on top of the Paisley rug that covered his knees.

'We are trying to establish some facts regarding the dead man's character and history. I wonder if you could help us? Did you engage him in conversation at all? He may, perhaps, have mentioned where he came from, or what he was doing in the town,' suggested Ravenscroft hopefully, although realizing that he was probably clutching at straws.

'The gentleman said very little as I recall. He had only been here for a short period of time before his sad demise. No, I am afraid we cannot assist you in this matter,' replied Jacobson.

'I see. How long have you and Mrs Jacobson resided here at Talbots'?' enquired Ravenscroft casting a brief glance round the dimly lit room, where to him it seemed as though time had stopped still many years ago.

'Five years,' said Mrs Jacobson.

'And before that?' asked Ravenscroft.

'London,' replied Jacobson. 'But why do you ask? I cannot see what this has to do with poor Mr Jones.'

'We believe that Mr Jones did not die from eating too much of the Brown Windsor, but rather that he was poisoned by someone in this house.'

'And you think that we may be suspects?' protested Jacobson, with a slight laugh.

'No, not at all. It would assist us in our inquiries, however if we could learn a little about each of the residents, so that they could be eliminated from our inquiries,' replied Ravenscroft attempting to sound as tactful as he could.

'I see, inspector. What would you like to know?' said Jacobson reaching out for his wife's hand.

'If you could tell us a little about your background, and how you came to live here in Pershore?' asked Ravenscroft. 'I believe you may originate from abroad?'

'You are correct, inspector. My husband came originally from St. Petersburg,' said Mrs Jacobson taking hold of her husband's hand.

'I left there twenty-five years ago, to escape the persecution that I was subject to in that city. We Jews were not welcome there, and were encouraged to leave,' replied Jacobson. 'It is not easy living in a country where the ruling powers do not like you, but then Jews have often been disliked in the countries where we have settled. And so I came to London. I was a professor of Religious Studies at the Saint Petersburg University, so I was able to secure some employment in a Jewish teaching establishment in London. Fortunately you English are a more tolerant race of people.'

'And you, Mrs Jacobson?' asked Ravenscroft addressing the young woman. 'You are not Jewish, I presume?'

'You are correct, inspector. I was bought up in Whitechapel in London. I was a seamstress by occupation. Then one day I met my husband,' replied the woman smiling some-what nervously.

'Crosskeys Lodging House was where we met, was it not, my dear?' added Jacobson.

'I know Whitechapel very well,' said Ravenscroft.

75

'Then you will know why we left shortly after our marriage. All that noise, and smells, and over-crowding. My eyesight was beginning to fade. Rosanna here suggested that we should move elsewhere, and so it was that our searches bought us here eventually to Pershore. It is a pleasant enough town. Talbots' is not the best of establishments, as I think you will quickly discover, inspector, but it serves our needs and we live very frugally.'

'Is that all, inspector?' asked the old man's wife abruptly. 'I think we have answered all your questions. Now my husband needs his rest.'

'Yes, thank you,' said Ravenscroft rising from his seat. 'You have both been very helpful.'

'I will see you out,' said Mrs Jacobson.

'I do not suppose that either of you sent me a letter concerning the death of Jones?' asked Ravenscroft.

'No. Why would we have done that?' replied Jacobson.

'It is of no consequence. Thank you once again for your time.'

* * *

'Well, they are an odd couple,' whispered Crabb as the two men stood on the landing.

'Yes. It is apparent that the old man is very much dependent on his young wife for most things, although I wonder if he is really as blind as he says he is?' replied Ravenscroft.

'What drives a young woman like that to marry such an old man as him?'

'I don't know. There is certainly a great deal of difference in their ages. She must be in her twenties, whereas he must be well into his seventies I would think. I wonder why they married, and why did he marry a Christian?'

'She came from Whitechapel. Your old territory, sir,' laughed Crabb. 'Seamstress she said.'

'And so she might have been, who knows. She seemed very unsettled by our presence, and very protective of her husband, but then perhaps that is understandable. Did you notice how she blushed when he mentioned the Crosskeys Lodging House?'

'Yes sir,' replied Crabb.

'Well, I know the Crosskeys. It was a place frequented by certain ladies of the night.'

'My word, sir! No wonder she went red when you mentioned that you knew Whitechapel.'

'It may be nothing of course.'

'You think they may have killed Jones?' asked Crabb.

'I cannot see an obvious motive, although

they could have encountered Jones in London before they came here I suppose. I feel they may have a great deal more to tell us, but we will leave it for the present until we have interviewed all the other guests.'

'Shall I knock on this door?'

'If you would, Tom.'

Crabb raised his hand to the door, but before he could bring it down on the panel, he found that it had suddenly opened.

'Ah, and you must be Inspector Ravenhill?' pronounced a tall, thin, upright grey-haired lady standing in the doorway.

'Ravenscroft. Detective Inspector Ravenscroft — and this is my associate Constable Crabb,' said the detective somewhat taken aback by the dramatic opening of the door.

'Inspector Ravenscroft, do please forgive me. Do come in inspector. We have heard so much about you from Mr Talbot. You have come about poor Mr Jones no doubt?' said the lady indicating that the two men should enter.

'Indeed, Miss Fanshaw,' replied Ravenscroft stepping into the room. 'I believe you and your sister may be able to assist us in our inquiries.'

'Do you hear that, Clarisa? The inspector says that we may be of assistance,' said the lady turning to face a frail, grey-haired woman, of even slighter stature, who rose from a chair before the fire.

'Good day to you, miss,' said Ravenscroft addressing the other woman. 'I understand that you are Miss Clarisa Fanshaw — and you are?' he asked turning to face the lady who had opened the door to them.

'Miss Arabella Fanshaw.'

'I am pleased to make your acquaintance, ladies.'

'Do please take a seat, inspector,' indicated his hostess. 'Perhaps you and your constable would like some tea?'

'That would be most kind of you,' replied Ravenscroft accepting the chair near the fire, as the two sisters left the room.

'Very pleasant,' whispered Crabb taking one of the other chairs.

Ravenscroft looked around the room with its comfortable armchairs, patterned carpet, Regency sideboard and delicate ornaments, and could not help feeling the contrast with the previous room he had just visited. Whereas the Jacobsons' room had a darkened, almost claustrophobic atmosphere, this room evidenced much light and warmth, and displayed a care and attention to detail of its occupants. A painting of a small Georgian country house, set in woodland, hung in centre place over the fireplace, and the mantel itself was adorned by old photographs of numerous people in ornate silver frames.

'Now here we are,' said Arabella Fanshaw returning to the room bearing a large silver tray, closely followed by her sister, after a few minutes had elapsed.

'Allow me, miss,' said Crabb standing up and taking hold of the tray.

'Thank you, constable,'

'Where would you like me to place it, miss?'

'On the table over there by the chair, if you will.'

'You have delightful rooms here,' said Ravenscroft. 'You must have been here for quite a while?'

'Ten years,' said the younger sister speaking for the first time.

'Twelve, my dear Clarisa, if I am not mistaken,' corrected Arabella.

'So you have not always lived in Pershore?' asked Ravenscroft glancing across at the painting.

'No, we came originally from Ireland, near Coleraine,' offered Clarisa.

'How do you like your tea, inspector,' interrupted Arabella turning to face Ravenscroft.

'Just a little milk and sugar.'

'And you, constable?'

'The same miss, thank you', replied Crabb.

'Now how can my sister and I be of assistance to you?' asked Arabella after Ravenscroft and Crabb had been handed their cups. 'We were given to understand that poor Mr Jones died from eating too much of that dreadful soup that Mrs Talbot cooked for us all. We were both quite ill ourselves in the night.'

'That is what we first thought, but new evidence has come to light which suggests that Mr Jones was in fact poisoned,' replied Ravenscroft.

'Oh, good heavens!' exclaimed the younger sister with a look of alarm.

'Now then, Clarisa, do not distress yourself. Go on, inspector,' said the anxious elder sister.

'In fact it appears that Mr Jones did not in fact partake of the soup during the dinner. We believe that poison had been placed in his bottle of tawny port.'

'How perfectly awful,' said the younger sister turning away.

'How perfectly dreadful. Who can have done such a terrible thing?' added Arabella.

'That is what we would like to know. Can either of you ladies provide us with any information regarding the dead man? Did he ever speak to you, or confide in you perhaps?'

'No, Mr Jones said very little. Of course, he was only with us for just under two weeks. I don't think he wanted to talk to anyone very much. Not a sociable kind of person at all. We did try to engage him in conversation, but he expressed little interest,' replied Arabella with a slight hint of disapproval.

'Do you recall if he spoke with anyone else in particular?' continued Ravenscroft.

'No. There was no one.'

'Did he ever give any indication what his business was here in Pershore, or where he might have originated?'

'I think he — ,' began the younger sister.

'Mr Jones did mention that he would only be with us for a short time,' interrupted Arabella.

'Did he say where he might be going to when he left this establishment?' asked Ravenscroft sipping his tea.

'He might have mentioned once that he was waiting for a letter which might take him shortly to London,' offered Arabella.

'That is interesting — and do you know whether he received such a letter?'

'I don't know. If he did, he certainly did not mention it.'

'Did Mr Jones ever give any indication that he had previously been known to any of the residents of Talbots'?'

'What a strange question to ask, inspector,' smiled Arabella.

'It may be that the deceased gentleman had previously encountered one of the residents here sometime in the past, and that this other person may have had a reason to poison him.'

'How extraordinary. More tea, inspector?'

'No thank you, Miss Fanshaw. So there was no one in particular whom you saw conversing with Mr Jones?'

'No one,' said Clarisa in a quiet voice and with a vacant expression.

'No one,' echoed Arabella, 'Although there was one occasion I recall, about three or four days ago, when I happened to be on the landing one evening, and I saw Mr Jones and Miss Martin conversing together at the foot of the stairs. Of course they may have been exchanging casual gossip about the weather. They were speaking in hushed tones together and I know that when they observed me Miss Martin seemed somewhat agitated, and quickly moved away and entered the dining room alone.'

'I see. That is most interesting, Miss Fanshaw,' said Ravenscroft looking up at Crabb who was making notes in his pocket book.

'You did not mention that to me,' said Clarisa.

'Of course I did, Clarisa. I mentioned it to you later that same evening. It is just that you have forgotten, as usual. I expect it was all rather innocent,' added Arabella.

'I am sure you are correct. We have yet to interview Miss Martin. Finally, can either of you good ladies think why anyone at Talbots' would have wanted Mr Jones dead?'

'No. No one at all. All this is quite terrible, inspector. We simply cannot believe that anyone would have wanted to poison poor Mr Jones,' said Arabella. 'Certainly no one here.'

'I thought he was quite a nice man,' added Clarisa.

'I am sure we will not sleep easily in our beds, inspector, until you have caught the person who has committed this terrible deed.'

'I expect we will soon be able to discover whoever is responsible for this dark deed,' said Ravenscroft placing his cup on the table and rising to his feet. 'Thank you so much for the tea. Rest assured, ladies, we will do everything we can to apprehend the perpetrator.'

'I do hope so, inspector,' said Arabella as she and her sister rose from their seats.

'I wish you good day, ladies. You have been most helpful,' said Ravenscroft as he and Crabb were shown through the door.

'Well they seem a couple of nice ladies,' remarked Crabb after the door had been closed behind them. 'Wouldn't say boo to a goose.'

Ravenscroft smiled. 'It is no use our calling upon Mr Claybourne at present, as both the maid and Talbot said that he was away in London. So, I think we will go upstairs and see if we can find Miss Martin.'

Ravenscroft and Crabb retraced the steps of their previous visit and found themselves again on the second-floor landing where the dead man, Jones, had lodged, and knocked on the door opposite.

'Good morning. Miss Martin, I presume?' asked Ravenscroft addressing the tall, slim, young lady who opened the door to them. 'My name is Ravenscroft, Inspector Ravenscroft. I wonder if I might have a few words with you regarding the late Mr Jones?'

'Yes of course. Mr Talbot mentioned that you had called yesterday,' replied the woman leading the way into the small sitting room. 'Do please sit down, inspector.'

Ravenscroft accepted the chair and glanced briefly round the simply furnished room.

'I was given to understand from Talbot that poor Mister Jones had died through eating too much of the soup,' said Miss Martin sitting down on a blue, buttonbacked sewing chair and looking directly at Ravenscroft over the top of her spectacles.

'That is what we were led to believe yesterday, but new evidence has come to light to suggest that Mr Jones was deliberately poisoned,' said Ravenscroft.

'That is awful — but how?'

'Someone put poison in his tawny, miss,' said Crabb.

'How terrible, but I don't understand, why would anyone do such a thing?' asked the young woman quickly rising from the chair, and walking across to the window, where she looked anxiously through the glass.

'That is what we would like to find out,' said Ravenscroft.

'But he was such a nice gentleman. Poison, you said? I cannot comprehend such a deed.'

'Forgive me, Miss Martin, I did not wish to cause you any alarm. May I ask if you had formed some attachment to the said gentleman?' asked Ravenscroft rather hesitantly.

'No. No, of course I had not. I had only known Mr Jones for just under two weeks. We had conversed once or twice together, that is all. Why do you ask such a question?' asked Miss Martin.

'It is just that Miss Fanshaw recalled you

and Mr Jones talking together on the landing one evening,' said Ravenscroft realizing that if he was to arrive at the truth regarding the relationship he would have to be more forthright in his questioning.

'I do not recall such a conversation. Miss Fanshaw must be mistaken. The only time when I spoke with Mr Jones was at the dinner table when others were present,' replied Miss Martin abruptly turning round to face Ravenscroft.

'So you cannot provide us with any information, miss, regarding the said gentleman?' asked Crabb.

'No.'

'He never spoke of where he had lived before his arrival here, or where he intended going in the future?' asked Ravenscroft.

'No. I have told you that Mr Jones did not confide in me,' said the lady resuming her seat and placing her hands tightly together on her lap.

'There has been talk of a letter,' said Ravenscroft leaning forwards. 'Apparently Mr Jones was awaiting delivery of a letter.'

'I know of no such letter. Mr Jones did not mention anything about a letter to me.'

'Can you think of anyone at Talbots' who might have borne a grudge against Mr Jones?'

'No. As I said Mr Jones was a very quiet

man. He kept very much to himself. I would not have known if he had any enemies.'

'Did you ever observe Mr Jones in conversation with any of the other residents?' continued Ravenscroft.

'No. As I said, he kept very much to himself.'

'May I ask how long you have lived here at Talbots' Miss Martin?' asked Ravenscroft.

'Why do you ask such a question? It surely cannot have any relevance to the death of Mr Jones.'

'We are just trying to find out as much as we can about the residents here,' said Ravenscroft, feeling somewhat disconcerted by the young lady's offhand manner.

'Because you believe that one of us may have poisoned Mr Jones?'

'Indeed, Miss Martin. Someone in this house put poison in Mr Jones's drink, and Constable Crabb and I have a duty to reveal and apprehend the culprit.'

'I see. Well, to answer your question, inspector, I have resided here for the past three years. I have a small annuity left to me by my aunt which enables me to live a comfortable, but careful existence. Now, if that is all I can tell you . . . ' said Miss Martin rising quickly from her seat.

'What can you tell me about the other

guests here?' asked Ravenscroft.

'I do not see that it is my concern to pass any comment on other people.'

'It would greatly help us in our inquiries, Miss Martin, if you could assist us in this matter,' persisted Ravenscroft.

'The two Miss Fanshaws have lived here the longest. Professor Jacobson came originally from Russia I believe, and his wife from London. Mr Claybourne is a commercial gentleman and is only with us for two or three days each week. Count Turco is a musician from Italy, and Mr Cherrington I know little of as he has only been with us for a few weeks. That is all I can tell you, Inspector Ravenscroft.'

'And Talbot?' asked Ravenscroft keen to observe the other's reaction.

'I have little to do with either Mr Talbot or his wife,' replied Miss Martin turning away from Ravenscroft and looking directly across towards the window once more.

'Thank you, Miss Martin,' said Ravenscroft rising to his feet. 'I appreciate your assistance.'

'I will show you out, inspector. I still cannot comprehend why anyone here would have wanted Mr Jones dead.'

'Well someone did, miss,' said Crabb.

'Thank you again, Miss Martin,' said Ravenscroft as he and Crabb left the room.

'She's hiding something, sir,' whispered Crabb after the door had been closed.

'I think you are correct, Tom. She was certainly very defensive in her answers. I think she knows more about the dead man than she is telling us, and did you see how she turned away when I mentioned Talbot. You may recall that Mrs Talbot hinted that her husband may have had some association with Miss Martin.'

'Young lady all alone like that, with limited means, must feel vulnerable at times.'

'Yes. I wonder why she has never married? Plain, but not unattractive, probably in her late twenties. Not unnatural that she could have been drawn towards our Mr Jones,' said Ravenscroft.

'Anyone would have been an improvement on Talbot,' added Crabb.

'I wonder what brought her here to Pershore? And if Talbot had been making unwelcome advances towards Miss Martin, why then did she not just leave?'

'Limited funds?' suggested Crabb. 'Talbots' is cheap.'

'You are probably right.'

'Shall we go back and question her more?'

'No, we will leave that until we have

interviewed the other guests. We still have one more flight. Listen, I think I can hear the sound of a violin being played,' said Ravenscroft.

'Sounds a bit sad to me,' remarked Crabb.

The two men followed the plaintive melody up the winding creaking staircase until they found themselves on a narrow darkened landing.

'This must be where the musician Turco resides,' said Ravenscroft banging on one of the two doors.

The music ceased and was shortly followed by the abrupt opening of the door.

'Who is it that dares to disturb the wonderful tunes of the glorious maestro Paganini?' enquired a bearded man glaring at Ravenscroft.

'I trust I have the honour of addressing Count Turco,' replied Ravenscroft. 'Forgive the intrusion, count.'

'Music is a sacred thing, sir. He who violates its flow has-a no inner feeling,' said the man brandishing a violin bow in the detective's direction.

'My name is Inspector Ravenscroft. This is my colleague Constable Crabb. We would like a few words with you regarding the late Mr Jones. If you could spare us some minutes of your time, we would be obliged.'

The musician flung open the rest of the door, and with a flourish indicated that the two policemen should enter.

Ravenscroft found himself in a near empty room where the only contents appeared to be a collection of music scores scattered around the floor, and a music stand which took centre place on a faded Turkish mat which had seen better days. The man's wayward black hair, piercing green eyes and dirty bottle-green waistcoat and grubby breeches seemed to complement the spartan surroundings.

'And what would you-a like to know?' snapped the occupant.

'You are aware that your fellow lodger Mr Jones was poisoned?' began Ravenscroft.

'That awful soup! I told them the soup was bad. They dare to call it a soup! This English food it is so bad, so bad!' exclaimed Turco waving his violin in the air before leaning it against a wall.

'No, it was not the soup. We have reason to believe that someone put poison in Mr Jones's port.'

'Hah! So it was not-a the soup at all. Perhaps it should have been. I know nothing of any poison. Now you-a go, and leave me with the beautiful Paganini. Yes?'

'I wonder if you could tell us anything

about the deceased man?' asked Ravenscroft ignoring the last request.

'Bah! Signor Jones, he-a no like my playing. He complain. Said I play too loudly, and that he could not sleep at night. He not appreciate good music. He should be glad I play. People pay good money to hear Turco play.'

'So you had words with Mr Jones?' asked Ravenscroft becoming interested in the Italian's replies.

'I-a close the door on him when he complain! No one else, they no complain. Signor Cherrington opposite he no complain. Miss Martin below, she no complain. Talbot he no complain. So why does Jones complain? I do not understand this man. He has no soul. Where is his soul, I ask you?'

'Gone to heaven now, sir,' Crabb could not help remarking.

'No, signor, he is-a not with the angels! Angels they like-a music. They would not want him. Let the devil have him. He would be good company for the Devil. Devil not like-a music.'

Ravenscroft smiled. 'Did you and Mr Jones ever come to blows?'

'Blows! I am not a man of violence, sir. Turco, he is a peaceful man. He come from Naples. The Turcos of-a Naples they are not a violent race. Turcos-a love Napoli! They love

93

the sun, and the pasta, and above all the music. Above all Turco he love Paganini!' continued Turco gradually becoming more animated.

'Did you ever speak with Mr Jones about anything else?'

'I-a not speak with Jones. Turco he not concern himself with such people!'

'Did you see anyone tampering with the bottle of port on the night he died?' asked Ravenscroft changing his line of questioning.

'No. I see no one. Turco he see-a nothing.'

'Did you at any time see Mr Jones in conversation with anyone else in the house?'

'No. Jones he is no concern of mine. I not concerned who talk with him. No one talk with him. He has no soul.'

'When did you come to this country, count?' enquired Ravenscroft, intrigued to discover more about the musician's history.

'Turco he leave his beloved Napoli twenty years ago. Why, I ask myself? Why do I come here and stay in this God-forsaken country? Is it the food? No, food is too cold and tasteless. Is it the weather? No, weather is bad. Always it-a rains. The sun, he often disappears. Why is it always winter here?'

'So why do you stay, sir?' asked Crabb.

'I stay for the music. It is the music that keeps me here.'

'And where do you play, sir?' asked Ravenscroft.

'You have not heard of the great Turco? Turco, the famous violinist. The man of a thousand melodies,' boasted the musician.

'I am afraid not,' replied Ravenscroft.

'I play in Birmingham, at the Town Hall, with the great orchestras. I go to London and play with the orchestras there. I go to Liverpool and I play there. Everywhere Turco he is in great demand. The people they applaud the great Turco. They like-a my playing. They want for nothing more, and Turco he gives the people what they want. They love my Paganini. They love Turco. Paganini and I, we make them cry, we make them laugh, we make them smile.'

'And how long have you lived here at Talbots', count?' interrupted Ravenscroft.

'I live here for past five years.'

'You have never thought of moving elsewhere?' suggested Ravenscroft.

'I have my violin. I have my music. Turco he want for nothing else.'

'Well thank you, count. We will leave you to continue with your music. Apologies for the interruption,' said Ravenscroft beginning to take his leave.

'You catch this infidel who poison this Jones?'

'We intend to do our very best, sir.'

'I no kill Jones. He no like my music, but Turco he is not a murderer,' protested the violinist.

'No one suggested that you were, sir,' said Ravenscroft. 'Good day to you. Oh, one more thing, count. Did you send me a letter concerning the death of Mr Jones?'

'What letter? Turco he no send letters to anyone!' said the violinist with a final gesture as he closed the door.

★ ★ ★

'Well, he is a queer fish and no mistake,' remarked Crabb as he and Ravenscroft stood on the landing once more.

'Those Italians can sometimes be quite excitable.'

'You think he poisoned Jones?'

'Why, because our Mr Jones did not like his playing? Perhaps, but probably not. One thing I found very strange though. If Turco is as famous a musician as he makes out, playing everywhere from London to Birmingham and Liverpool, why is he still living in such a down-at-heel place as this? No, I think our Count Turco is prone to exaggeration. Either that or he is not all that he makes himself out to be. Anyway, let's try and interview this Mr

Cherrington and see what we can find out about him,' said Ravenscroft tapping on the other door.

Receiving no reply, Ravenscroft repeated the action.

'Seems as though he is out, sir,' said Crabb.

'I think you must be correct, Tom. We will need to come back later. Wait a moment, who is that coming up the stairs?'

'Who is there?' called out a voice from the second-floor landing.

'Mr Cherrington?' asked Ravenscroft.

'Yes, who wants him?'

'We are the police, sir. We would like a word with you concerning the late Mr Jones.'

The man said nothing as he climbed the stairs.

'Good day to you, sir,' said Ravenscroft observing that the middle-aged bearded man carrying a silver cane was immaculately dressed with a red carnation and gold tie pin. 'My name is Detective Inspector Ravenscroft and this is Constable Crabb. We are making inquiries regarding the late Mr Jones and believe that you may be of some assistance to us.'

The man stared at Ravenscroft for a moment. 'Yes, of course. A terrible business. I will of course help you all I can. Perhaps you would like to go inside?'

'That is most kind of you, sir.'

Cherrington opened the door and led the way into a poorly furnished room.

'I am afraid it is not particularly salubrious here,' smiled Cherrington. 'But then you know what Talbots' is like.'

'I gather you have not been long resident here, sir?' said Ravenscroft accepting a chair by the table in the centre of the room, that the other had indicated.

'Two to three months. Of course, I do not intend remaining here for much longer. All a question of waiting for my funds to arrive. Do you smoke, inspector?' asked Cherrington offering Ravenscroft a cigarette from a gold case. 'Got them on the boat back from India from a man who had just returned from Turkey.'

'No thank you, sir.'

'You would not object if I . . . ?'

'Of course not, sir.'

Cherrington lit a cigarette, seated himself in a large leather armchair before the empty fireplace and inhaled deeply. 'Been out in India for the past five years. Still waiting for my goods and chattels to arrive. Bit of a nuisance doing without things. Not used to doing without. Can't really move on. But enough of that. How can I be of assistance, inspector?'

'You were in the Indian army, sir?' enquired Ravenscroft.

'Good heavens no! Tea. That's what I was involved in. Tea. Had a plantation near Darjeeling,' replied Cherrington leaning back in the armchair and blowing smoke out into the room.

'But you came back here to England?' continued Ravenscroft interested in knowing more of the man's history.

'Got rather bored with it out there. Nothing to do in the evenings, but go to the local clubhouse. Full of noisy army types always talking about polo and tiger shooting. Decided to sell up and come back home to the old country. There's nothing like England is there? You ever lived abroad Ravenscroft?'

'No, sir.'

'Travelled all over the world I have. New York, Jo'burg, Cairo, Bombay, even Sydney, but England is still the best place to be. My rambling days are over. Hope to put down some roots now.'

'You have no family, sir?'

'Wife died in India about two years ago,' replied Cherrington stroking his well groomed beard.

'Oh, I'm sorry.'

'Damn fever carried her off. Not a good place India; climate is too damned hot, too many flies, people dying all over the place — but then I don't expect you are interested in all that. I expect you want to know more about poor old Jones. Died of eating too much of that soup so they said. Didn't have any affect on me, although I believe most of the others were ill. Poor man. Must have had a delicate constitution.'

'We have since discovered that Mr Jones was poisoned. Someone apparently put poison in his bottle of port,' said Ravenscroft watching Cherrington to see what affect this disclosure would have on him.

'Good Lord! Whoever would want to go and do a thing like that?'

'Who indeed, Mr Cherrington? That is what we have come to investigate.'

'Yes, well I can see that. Poisoned you say? Well, I am surprised,' replied Cherrington before taking another puff on his cigarette.

'Oh, why do you say that?'

'Well, can't see why anyone would want to kill him like that. He seemed quite a pleasant sort of fellow. Bit on the quiet side. I didn't have much opportunity to speak to him of course, but he struck me as being quite inoffensive and reserved.'

'Did Mr Jones tell you anything of his history, or what he might be doing in the future?'

'No, I don't think so. As I said, he wasn't the sort of man you could have a long conversation with. Played his cards close to his chest, if you see what I mean.'

'Can you think of anyone here who would have wanted him dead?' asked Ravenscroft.

'No. I can't see either of the Miss Fanshaws, or straight-laced Miss Martin, killing him, nor that mad Italian, or the miserable old professor,' laughed Cherrington.

'And Mr Claybourne?' asked Crabb.

'Now there's a mystery man if ever there was one. Claims to be some sort of commercial traveller, although what he is supposed to be selling I have no idea. Just seems to be here for two or three days each week. Where he goes to the rest of the time, I don't know. I suppose he might be your man.'

'And Mr and Mrs Talbot?' suggested Ravenscroft.

'Talbot!' exclaimed Cherrington. 'That man is afraid of his own shadow. Completely under the thumb of that wife of his. He reminds me of a greasy fly waiting to be swatted. I suppose there is always the possibility that she could have killed poor old Jones. Perhaps she was repulsed by his amorous intentions or he complained about the cooking?'

'Now I think you are jesting, Mr Cherrington,' replied Ravenscroft. 'Well sir, I think that will be all for now.'

'Oh, is that all? I was quite enjoying our little chat,' said Cherrington rising from his chair.

'We may need to question you again, sir.'

'Anytime, inspector.'

'I do not suppose you are the author of a letter sent to me regarding Jones's death?'

'No. Why the devil would I want to do such a thing?' laughed Cherrington.

'I take it you won't be leaving Talbots' in the next week or so?'

'Alas, no. As I said, waiting for my funds to arrive, then I shall put Talbots' behind me as I head off once more to the capital. Catch up with a few friends, maybe buy a nice little place in Primrose Hill or Highgate. Yes, that would be nice. Can't understand why they are taking so long. Then again the world of finance can often proceed at an annoyingly slow pace.'

★   ★   ★

'Well, Tom, what do you make of our Mr Cherrington?' asked Ravenscroft as he and Crabb walked back to their trap.

'Rather a smooth character if you ask me,' answered Crabb.

'Yes, he had quite a disarming manner. I

102

don't believe he has been out in India for the past five years.'

'Oh, why do you say that, sir?'

'A man who has just returned from growing tea in India would have had a much darker complexion. I would be surprised if Mr Cherrington has got any further than the white cliffs of Dover. Although well dressed, with an expensive cane and gold cigarette case, I don't believe that he is waiting for any funds to arrive. There probably aren't any funds, that's why he is reduced to staying at Talbots'. I could be wrong of course. I could be doing the man a grave injustice. Did you notice how he quickly suggested Claybourne as a possible murderer?'

'Yes, but difficult to know whether he was being serious or not.'

'He was certainly amusing regarding Mrs Talbot. She may be a formidable woman, but I can't see her killing Jones, can you?'

'No sir.'

'How old do you think our Mr Cherrington is, Tom?'

'Probably about thirty-five sir.'

'I think I would put him as being much older than that, perhaps nearly fifty.'

'Difficult to tell underneath that black beard and moustache.'

'Yes. He takes a great pride in his

appearance. I tell you something though, Tom. I had quite a distinct impression that I have seen our Mr Cherrington somewhere before, but I can't for the life of me remember where, and when . . . '

4

Ledbury

Ravenscroft poured himself out another glass of sherry and stirred the dying embers of his fire with the brass poker. He noted that the grandfather clock showed fifteen minutes past twelve, before once more going over in his mind the events of the previous day.

He had hoped that his visit to Talbots' Lodging House would have made clear why Jones had been poisoned, and that an early arrest could have been made, but instead his inquiries had only resulted in a deepening of the mystery. With no body, and no items of a personal nature remaining from the deceased man, Ravenscroft knew that he had very little to assist him in his investigations. Just who was Jones — if that was his real name — and what had he been doing at Talbots'? During his short time there he had apparently said little to his fellow guests. Everyone had remarked on how the man had liked to keep his own counsel. There was mention that he had been waiting for a letter to arrive. Had Jones received such a missive before his death, and if he had, why had he not then moved on? Had the fragment recovered by Crabb from beneath the man's bed been part of such a letter?

Then there was the question of how Jones had been killed. Clearly it had not been the Brown Windsor, for, although all the other diners had been made ill through eating the soup, they had all recovered fully, but then of course Jones had not taken that dish at all. The mysterious letter that Ravenscroft had received claimed that poison had been placed in Jones's tawny port bottle, from which only he had drunk, and the killer had made sure that the bottle had been removed promptly after the dinner in question, thereby destroying the evidence. The poison, however must have been of the slow-acting variety as the man had not collapsed immediately after drinking it, but had gone straight up to his room, where he had died in his bed sometime during the night.

So, who had killed Jones? And why? Could robbery have been the motive? Did Jones own certain valuables that the killer would have taken after the man had died? If that was the case, then suspicion must fall on Talbot. The maid, Maisie, had said that Talbot had cleared the room of the dead man's effects, and Talbot himself had admitted that he had thrown the items away, but Ravenscroft had felt that the landlord had not been telling him the truth. There must have been some property that Talbot had appropriated for himself. He would have to question the man again, for he knew that if he were to find out more about Jones and eliminate a false identity, then he would need to recover and examine those personal items.

So, had Talbot poisoned his guest to acquire Jones's valuables? But then did Talbot seem like a killer? There was certainly something rather grubby and underhand about the man. He had played down his wife's boast that he had served in the Crimea, and then there had been that suggestion that he had had some kind of a relationship in the past with Miss Martin. If that had been the case, then perhaps Jones had somehow uncovered this indiscretion, and the two men had quarrelled — but then, as Ravenscroft reminded himself, he was in danger of letting his imagination play tricks with his reasoning.

If Talbot had not poisoned Jones, either for financial gain, or in a pique of temper, then who had? He could rule out both the maid, Maisie — after all it was she who had alerted Ravenscroft to the case, through Stebbins — and Mrs Talbot, who clearly had no reason to kill her lodger. That just left the eight lodgers. One of them must have killed Jones, but which one — and why?

He had first interviewed the old Jewish professor, Jacobson, and his young wife. Could they have poisoned Jones? Jacobson had arrived in England some years ago, after choosing to leave his homeland in Russia where he claimed that he had been persecuted. Whilst in London he had met the youthful Rosanna, and the two had married, arriving at Talbots' five years ago. Could there have been something in either of the couples' past histories that linked them to Jones? No one had suggested that Jones had been Russian, so it was unlikely that he had originated from there, but could he have been some former lover of the woman? Jacobson had accidentally let slip that the couple met whilst Rosanna had been staying at the Crosskeys Lodging House in Whitechapel. Ravenscroft knew from his days of police service in that area that Crosskeys was not the kind of establishment where young ladies of virtue resided. Could Jones have been a former client of the woman — and if so, could she have poisoned him to prevent her secret being revealed to her husband? But then Jacobson must have known about his wife's dark past, so perhaps Jacobson himself poisoned the man, to protect his wife?

Jacobson claimed to be blind, but maybe that was a feint, and he could really see more that he claimed. Either way the couple seemed something of a mystery. Why had she married a man so much older than herself — and why had that room been so dull, so full of gloom and lost hope?

Ravenscroft next considered the Fanshaw sisters. Arabella, the eldest, seemed the more dominant of the two, she clearly saw herself as the younger sibling's protector. They were the oldest residents at Talbots', having lived there for some ten years or more. Why had they never moved on to more pleasant surroundings? Was there something in their past that had kept them at the run-down lodging house? Could they have met Jones many years ago?

Then there was Miss Martin. Mrs Talbot had hinted of some kind of relationship between her husband and her lodger, and Miss Fanshaw had observed Miss Martin and Jones talking in low whispers on the landing one evening. Had she known Jones in the past, a former lover perhaps who had caused her great harm at that time, and whom she had now killed as an act of personal revenge? That was a possibility. Miss Martin had certainly adopted a defensive manner during his questioning. Why had she never married?

In her late twenties, she was far from being unattractive, and if Talbot had made unwelcome advances towards her, why had she not left the lodging house rather than stay in a place where she would have seen the man day in and day out? Ravenscroft knew that he would need to question the spinster further if he were to obtain the truth.

Next there was the Italian violinist, Count Turco. He had claimed that Jones had complained about his playing and that there had been some kind of argument between the two men. The Italian behaved as though he possessed a volatile temperament. Could he have killed Jones in a rush of temper? Death by poisoning required careful planning however, and then again if Turco had killed Jones in this way why would he have drawn attention to himself by telling the policemen about their disagreement? Ravenscroft could see no obvious reason why Turco would have committed the crime, but there was something about the man that did not quite ring true. Was he really a Count? Did he even come from Italy? And had he been exaggerating when he claimed to give concerts in London, Manchester and Birmingham? Surely such a great artist as that would not have been reduced to living in a half-empty room, in a cheap lodging house in Pershore. No, he was sure that Turco had not told him the truth, but did that deception make him a murderer?

Lastly there had been Cherrington, a flamboyant man who appeared to like the good things in life. What was he doing then living at Talbots'? Had he really just come back to the country after five years on a tea plantation in India? Was he really waiting for funds to arrive, as he claimed, so that he could move on to better things? Ravenscroft doubted that the man had ever left the country, and believed that the funds were a creation of an over-active mind always seeking to impress. Mrs Talbot had described him as a 'perfect gentleman' and on the surface that appeared to be true, but was the man merely putting on an act, seeking always to take centre stage and impress others? If the account of his past had been a true one, why would he then have come to a cheap lodging house, in a small country town, instead of finding more suitable, comfortable accommodation elsewhere? All of this of course did not make him the man who had poisoned Jones, unless the two men had known each other in the past, and Cherrington had taken it upon himself to remove his enemy in such a ruthless fashion. Could Jones have even been blackmailing Cherrington about a dubious past, threatening to expose him as a fraud. Was this why he had been silenced? That seemed a strong possibility. Was Cherrington just a man who liked to show off, or was there something more underhand about him? Cherrington was certainly a mystery, and the more he thought about the man, the more Ravenscroft was convinced that he had seen him somewhere before — but where, and in what circumstances? If only he could remember . . .

Then Ravenscroft realized that there was another suspect whom he had yet to interview — Claybourne, the commercial traveller, who had been absent during his two visits to the house. Just who was this Claybourne, and why did he rent a room there, and then occupy it for as little as two or three nights a week? Where did he originate, and was there really enough business in the town and its surrounding areas to warrant such an outlay of expenditure? If the man was using his room for so little time each week, would it not have been more prudent to stay at one of the nearby inns on the nights when he was resident in town? Was this Claybourne really a commercial traveller, and if so, what did he sell, or was this yet another kind of pretence, a mask for something more sinister? Ravenscroft knew that those questions could not be answered until the man returned, and until then he would have to keep an open mind.

So there they all were — a house full of possible suspects, each one appearing to have something to hide. A cheap lodging house where its inmates seemed to harbour strange secrets. The kind of establishment where people arrived with the sincere intention of staying for only a short period of time, until their circumstances changed for the better, but also a house from which its residents seemed unable to move away; the kind of house where dreams had long been abandoned, and where the past had almost eclipsed both the present and the future.

As Ravenscroft drained his glass and dampened down the fire, he knew that he would be returning to Pershore in the morning, and that his inquiries would continue there until he had unravelled those personal secrets, and had unmasked the quiet killer.

5

Pershore

'So we find ourselves once more in Pershore,' remarked Ravenscroft as he and Crabb alighted from the trap.

'What are we going to do today, sir?' asked the constable.

'More questions, I'm afraid. I think we both had the distinct impression yesterday that several of the lodgers at Talbots' were not exactly telling us the truth. I am convinced that one of them must have encountered Jones in the past, and that was why the man had to be silenced. The problem is, which one? Who do you think is our chief suspect, Tom?'

'Difficult to say, sir. As you said, they all appear to have something to hide, but if you ask me, I would say either that Miss Martin, or the Cherrington fellow.'

'Oh, why do you say that?'

'Well, I thought that Miss Martin was somewhat secretive and defensive in her answers. I reckoned she knew a lot more about Jones than she was prepared to tell us.'

'Good reasoning, Tom — and Mr Cherrington?'

'Rather too oily. Something about the man I did not like. I would certainly not trust him with the care of my grandmother. All wind and puff, or as we says in Worcestershire 'if he was born under a threepenny planet he'd never be worth fourpence'.'

'I'm inclined to agree with you,' smiled Ravenscroft. 'But I am sure I have seen the man somewhere before, and I just can't recall where.'

'You could have arrested him sometime during your time in Whitechapel, sir?' suggested Crabb.

'Maybe, but somehow I don't think so.'

'Is that not Mrs Jacobson on the other side of the road?' asked Crabb.

'I believe so. She certainly seems to be in a hurry. Without her husband I see. I wonder where she is going?'

'Then there is that Claybourne,' said Crabb returning to their discussion.

'Ah yes. The mysterious Claybourne. We certainly need to have a word or two with him. I wonder if he has returned yet?'

'Talk of the devil, sir. If I am not mistaken that is Mr Cherrington woffling along towards us now.'

'And looking very presentable and assured

he does with his carnation and walking stick.'

'Good morning, Ravenscroft. Lovely day to be out in the autumn sunshine, would you not agree, inspector?'

'It is indeed, Mr Cherrington,' acknowledged Ravenscroft.

'Thought I would take a stroll through the town and out towards the abbey. Never know whom you might meet. Have you made any progress with your inquiries?'

'Our investigations are proceeding at a satisfactory pace.'

'Splendid. Then we can look forwards to an early arrest?'

'And have your funds arrived yet from India?' enquired Ravenscroft, choosing to ignore the last question.

'Alas, no. Just visited the bank. Non-arrival, I'm afraid — but imminent, so one lives in expectation and hope. You know how things are?'

'I do indeed, Mr Cherrington.'

'Well, if you will excuse me, inspector?'

'Of course, sir. Enjoy your walk.'

'Oh, I'm sure I will. Good day to you both,' said Cherrington briefly raising his hat before striding off through the market place.

'Come, Tom, let us return to Talbots'. I think we would benefit from having a further conversation with the Fanshaw sisters.'

'Oh, why do you say that, sir?' asked Crabb.

'I expect that those two ladies know everything there is to know about the residents of Talbots'. Women of a certain age and standing make good observers, I find.'

★　★　★

'Good morning to you, Miss Fanshaw,' said Ravenscroft addressing the elder of the two sisters. 'Constable Crabb and I would be glad of a few more words with you both.'

'Who is it, dear?' called a voice from inside the room.

'It is that nice inspector and his young constable again,' replied Arabella.

'Oh, do show them in.'

Ravenscroft and Crabb entered the room.

'I trust I find you well, ladies?' asked Ravenscroft.

'Very well inspector, thank you,' replied Arabella. 'How may we be of assistance to you?'

'We were hoping that you could provide us with some information regarding your fellow lodgers.'

'Oh, what kind of information, inspector? I hope you do not assume that we are the sort of people who engage in idle gossip about our fellow guests?' said the older sister, a hint of reproach in the tone of her voice.

'Certainly not,' echoed Clarisa.

'Indeed not, ladies. I would not dare to suggest such a thing, as I know that you are both entirely above reproach on that score. It is just that you have both resided here longer than anyone else, and may be able to provide us with valuable insights regarding the behaviour and characters of your fellow guests,' said Ravenscroft seeking to placate the two women.

'You had better take a seat, inspector,' smiled Clarisa.

'Thank you.'

'Where would you like to start?' enquired Arabella.

'I wonder if we might begin with Professor Jacobson and his wife,' suggested Ravenscroft accepting the seat as Crabb stood by the door and took out his pocketbook.

'I don't think you should write any of this down,' said Clarisa looking anxiously in Crabb's direction.

'Of course not, miss. Crabb — if you will,' instructed Ravenscroft.

'Yes sir,' acknowledged Crabb, replacing the pocketbook in his tunic.

'Perhaps if your constable would also like to sit down,' suggested Arabella.

'Crabb, take that seat over there,' said Ravenscroft.

'Now you were asking about Professor Jacobson. Such a strange couple. I suppose you have noticed that she is so very much younger?' said Arabella, relieved that Crabb had assumed a less formal position in the room.

'I did indeed observe that,' replied Ravenscroft.

'Of course, we don't have very much to do with them. They are so very different from us. He comes from St. Petersburg, you know. He told us once of the terrible things they did there to people of the Jewish race. I suppose he was quite anxious to leave. He is quite a learned man by all accounts,' continued Arabella.

'And Mrs Jacobson?' asked Ravenscroft anxious to know more about the odd couple.

'Well she is certainly not Jewish,' remarked Arabella.

'I thought Jews could only marry Jews,' added Clarisa.

'I suppose they don't always have to. I believe they met in London. In Whitechapel I understand,' continued Arabella.

'Oh dear, wasn't that where all those terrible murders happened a few years ago?' asked the younger sister nervously.

119

'I believe they both left some three years before the murders took place,' interrupted Ravenscroft seeking to reassure the ladies.

'Oh that is a relief,' said Clarisa.

'Can you tell me anything about Mrs Jacobson?' asked Ravenscroft.

'I believe she comes from quite a lowly background. She was a seamstress, I gather. Such an odd thing for a man like him to marry a girl like that,' remarked Arabella.

'Did you ever observe either of them talking with Mr Jones?'

'No, I do not think so.'

'What do you know about the professor's blindness?'

'I don't quite understand you, inspector,' said the older sister.

'Professor Jacobson might not be as blind as he makes out, ladies,' suggested Crabb.

'Oh no, constable, he is quite blind, I can assure you. She has to lead him up the stairs and help serve his food. He is quite dependent upon her for everything,' continued Arabella.

'What can you tell me about Miss Martin?' asked Ravenscroft. 'You have already mentioned that you saw her and Mr Jones conversing together on the landing one evening.'

'My sister and I do not entirely approve of

Miss Martin,' replied Arabella adopting a more formal defensive tone.

'Oh, why is that?' asked Ravenscroft, keen to know more about their fellow lodger.

'Miss Martin likes to give the impression that she is quite alone and defenceless in this world, when in fact the opposite is true. Look at all that trouble with Talbot,' said Arabella.

'I think you are being rather harsh on poor Miss Martin, my dear,' said Clarisa.

'What can you tell me about Talbot and Miss Martin?' asked Ravenscroft leaning forwards in his seat and hoping that the two ladies would continue to be forthcoming in their observations of their fellow lodgers.

'I caught them kissing together on the landing one evening last year. It was quite unseemly,' announced Arabella.

'You never mentioned it to me,' said a startled Clarisa.

'I did not wish to upset you, my dear. Talbot is always going up to her room, on some pretext or other, delivering her post, taking up coals for her fire, that sort of thing.'

'I take it you do not approve of this, ladies?' suggested Ravenscroft.

'We certainly do not. He, a married man as well. I have seen her encouraging him. What does she want with a man like that, I ask you?' continued Arabella.

'Dear me, how terrible,' muttered the younger sister.

'A woman of her age should have acquired a husband of her own by now.'

'I am interested in Count Turco,' said Ravenscroft changing the subject of the conversation.

'A strange man,' said Arabella.

'But he plays such lovely tunes on his violin,' smiled Clarisa.

'He often entertains us in the evenings after dinner,' continued Arabella. 'The poor man. All of course is not what it seems.'

'Oh, why do you say that?' asked Ravenscroft his curiosity aroused.

'The Count is rather fond of the drink, to put it plainly. There have been times when he seemed quite unhappy with this world, and then he takes a bottle or two up to his room, and we do not see him for two, or even three days. All we can hear is the sound of that violin, so sad. Once I heard the poor man crying up there and there was the sound of furniture being knocked over, and shouting. It was all so distressing,' said Arabella shaking her head.

'So sad,' echoed Clarisa.

'Does the Count ever talk about his unhappiness?' asked Ravenscroft.

'No. After these dark periods, he usually

appears at breakfast the next day, being his usual excitable self,' replied Arabella.

'He did apologize once, I remember. He said it was the loneliness caused by his having left Italy and living in a strange country,' added Clarisa.

'They are so unpredictable these Italians,' said Arabella. 'I suppose it must be the result of all that sun.'

'Do you see much of Mr Claybourne?' asked Ravenscroft.

'He comes and goes. He is only here for one or two days a week,' offered Clarisa.

'Don't you find it strange, ladies, that Mr Claybourne would rent a room for such a short period of time each week?' continued Ravenscroft.

'Well, yes I suppose it is rather odd. I must say we have never thought about it like that. He is usually here on a Monday night,' said Arabella.

'And often on a Tuesday. Sometimes,' remarked the younger sister.

'I am given to understand that Mr Claybourne is some kind of commercial traveller?' asked Ravenscroft interested in knowing more about the absent lodger.

'Something very high up in insurance, I believe,' answered the older sister.

'Are you sure, my dear? I thought he was

something to do with the surveying of the roads,' suggested Clarisa.

'What on earth makes you think that? No, I am sure it is insurance. He is an agent for one of the large companies,' corrected Arabella.

'I thought I saw him coming into the house holding one of those round things in which you roll up a long measuring tape.'

'No Clarisa. It is insurance,' sighed Arabella.

'Insurance. I suppose you must be right, sister.'

'What about Mr Cherrington, miss?' asked Crabb.

'Oh, a real gentleman,' answered Arabella.

'So polite,' added Clarisa.

'Such an interesting gentleman. Always so entertaining at dinner. Why, only last week he was telling us all about his days in India. Did you know, inspector, that he used to grow tea in India, on the slopes of the hills, so enterprising,' smiled Arabella.

'Yes, he did mention it to us,' said Ravenscroft.

'Apparently he was once nearly eaten by a tiger!' exclaimed Arabella.

'Such a thrilling account!' added Clarisa.

'He was leading an expedition into the foothills, and it was just getting dark when a large angry tiger jumped out in front of the party and made to come towards them.'

'And what did Mr Cherrington do?' enquired Crabb.

'Apparently all the other members of the party ran away as fast as they could, but brave Mr Cherrington just stood his ground, and raised his rifle and shot the tiger straight between the eyes, just as the beast prepared to jump on him,' recounted Arabella becoming more and more animated.

'Such a thrilling story,' said Clarisa.

'Such a brave thing to have done, don't you think so, inspector?'

'Indeed, ladies,' agreed Ravenscroft.

'Such a pity that Mr Cherrington won't be staying with us for very much longer. The gentleman is waiting for his funds to arrive from India before returning to London,' said Arabella.

'So I believe,' smiled Ravenscroft. 'I wonder, did you ever observe Mr Cherrington and Mr Jones conversing together?'

'No. I don't think so. Did you ever notice them together, Clarisa?'

'No.'

'Thank you, ladies. I wonder if you would have a look at this letter for us,' said Ravenscroft retrieving the envelope from his inside pocket, which he had received the previous day, and handing it over to the two ladies to read. 'I wonder if perhaps you recognize the handwriting?'

The two sisters studied the contents of the letter intently.

'No, I am afraid we cannot help you, inspector,' said Arabella handing it back to Ravenscroft after some moments had elapsed.

'Thank you. Well, we will not take up any more of your time, ladies,' said Ravenscroft rising from the chair. 'I must say that you have a nice collection of old photographs and ornaments — and that portrait on the wall opposite is quite fine. Who is the young man?'

'Alas, that was poor Eustace, our brother,' replied Arabella.

'He died, about twenty years ago,' added Clarisa looking away, a sad expression on her face . . .

'I am sorry,' sympathized Ravenscroft. 'That must have been very upsetting for you both.'

'Yes. It was rather difficult, but you have to accept these things. There was nothing we could so. So you see, inspector, we are now quite alone in this world,' said Arabella shaking her head.

'We will always remember him though,' said the younger sister.

'Yes, of course,' said Ravenscroft realizing that his last question had caused some pain.

'I hope that we have been of some

assistance to you and your constable?' said Arabella recovering her composure.

'Indeed you have, ladies. You have been most enlightening. I cannot thank you enough,' said Ravenscroft.

'Let me show you out, inspector,' said Arabella walking over to the door.

'Do come again, inspector. We have so enjoyed your visit. It is not often that we get visitors,' smiled Clarisa.

'We will indeed. I wish you good day,' said Ravenscroft, as he and Crabb stepped out onto the landing.

★ ★ ★

'Delightful ladies,' remarked Crabb.

'Indeed, and most informative. They have provided us with several possible lines of inquiry. I think we will go and see Miss Martin next. I don't believe that she had only a passing acquaintance with the dead man, and I would certainly like to know more about her relationship with Talbot,' said Ravenscroft leading the way up the narrow staircase and onto the landing above.

'She was definitely hiding something from us, sir.'

Ravenscroft knocked on the door, but received no reply. 'Hum, she must be out at present. Let's ask the maid as I see she is just coming down the stairs.'

'Good morning, sir,' said Maisie.

'Good morning to you, miss. I wonder whether you have seen Miss Martin today?' asked Ravenscroft.

'No sir. She has not gone out as far as I know. She was not at breakfast either.'

'Is that unusual?'

'No, sir. Some of the guests do not always come down to breakfast. Shall I knock again for you, sir?'

Ravenscroft nodded, and the maid tapped on the wood.

'I think we should try to open the door,' suggested Ravenscroft pushing down the handle.

'You don't think something has happened to Miss Martin?' asked Maisie apprehensively.

'It may be better if I go in first,' suggested Ravenscroft slowly opening the door.

The two policemen entered the room, closely followed by the maid.

'Well Miss Martin does not appear to be in the sitting room. Let us try the bedroom,' said Ravenscroft crossing over the floor and opening the door to the inner room.

'Oh my God!' exclaimed Crabb bringing his hand up to his mouth.

The maid let out a loud scream, before falling to the floor.

6

Pershore

'See to the girl,' shouted Ravenscroft as he rushed over towards the bed.

'Here, miss, let me help you to this seat,' said Crabb assisting the maid to her feet, and guiding her back towards a chair in the sitting room . . .

Ravenscroft looked down on the deathly white figure lying prostrate on the floor by the side of the bed. 'I think Miss Martin has been poisoned. There is a glass on the floor which looks as though it must have slipped from her hand, and a half empty flagon of water on the bedside table.'

'Miss Martin,' mumbled the maid, a look of horror on her face. 'Is she . . . ?'

'I'm afraid so,' replied Ravenscroft retrieving the glass from the floor before smelling the contents of the flagon.

'Who could have done such a thing?' sobbed Maisie.

'Hum, there is no smell. Probably arsenic. No colour 'n' no doubt the same manner in which poor Jones was killed, but this must have been a much larger dose as it appears to have killed her quite quickly, although she was also violently sick. She must have taken a drink whilst sitting on the side of the bed, before intending to retire.'

'Don't distress yourself, miss,' said Crabb placing a hand on the girl's shoulder.

'Someone must have entered this room yesterday when Miss Martin was out and dropped the poison into the jug,' said Ravenscroft.

'Oh no, that was me, sir!' cried the maid.

'Whatever do you mean, Maisie?' asked Ravenscroft walking over towards the crying servant.

'It was me, sir! It was me that bought the water up here to Miss Martin late yesterday afternoon.'

'Yes that may be so Maisie, but I don't for one minute think that it was you who put poison in the flagon?' said Ravenscroft attempting to calm the servant's distress.

'No sir. I just poured the water out of the tap and brought it up here, as I always does,' replied the tearful maid.

'What time was that?' asked Ravenscroft.

'At about six, sir.'

'And was Miss Martin here when you entered the room?'

'No, sir.'

'And what did you do with the flagon?'

'I put it on the bedside table as I always do.'

'So someone must have entered the room afterwards, when Miss Martin was not here,' suggested Crabb.

'Or she entertained someone here in her room, someone who poured the poison into the flagon when she was not looking,' said Ravenscroft.

'But why Miss Martin?' asked the tearful maid looking upwards into Ravenscroft's face. 'Why would anyone want to harm her?'

'I don't know Maisie, but I can assure you that I intend to find out.'

'This is terrible!' exclaimed the maid before burying her tear-stained face in her hands.

'Crabb, would you be so kind as to escort Maisie downstairs. Tell the Talbots what has happened, but say that no one is to come up here,' instructed Ravenscroft.

'Yes, sir. Now you come along with me, miss,' said Crabb placing his arm round the servant's shoulder and assisting her towards the door.

'And, Tom, will you send a message to Doctor Homer and then make arrangements for the body to be taken to the mortuary.'

Crabb nodded as he and the sobbing maid left the room.

Ravenscroft knelt down on the floor and examined the body of the dead woman. A few minutes previously he had been anxious to interview the suspect, believing that the answers she might have provided would not only unravel the mystery of her relationships with Talbot and Jones, but would also have drawn him closer to the solution of the crime. Now, though, all that had been snatched away, leaving Ravenscroft with the realization that his task had just become increasingly difficult. If only he had trusted his instincts more, and questioned the woman more intently on their first meeting, perhaps then he would have arrived at the truth, Jones's murderer might now be in custody, and Miss Martin might still be alive.

Why would anyone have wanted to kill the woman? Had she been a party to Jones's death and been killed by her accomplice? Or had she known who the murderer was, and been poisoned to prevent her telling what she knew? Then of course there was another possibility — could Miss Martin have been Jones's killer? Had she become unsettled by Ravenscroft's questions and then decided to commit suicide rather than face the gallows? There seemed no way at present of proving which of these possibilities might be the correct one.

Ravenscroft rose to his feet and picked up the dead woman's spectacles, which he placed carefully on the bedside table. Then he set about examining the contents of the bedroom. A large wardrobe in the corner of the room revealed three dresses in its interior; they were plain, inexpensive items of attire that seemed to compliment their former owner's appearance. The small chest of drawers yielded other items of clothing.

Then Ravenscroft returned to the main room. A few books lay on the sidetable near the chair. He examined the various volumes and found them to be mainly anthologies of poetry and historical novels, before holding up the individual titles and shaking the pages to see if there were any letters or other personal jottings enclosed within. He then crossed to the writing desk where he saw an open book lying there, with a sheet of blue paper at its side, and upon closer examination he found the book to be a volume of John Keats's poems and that its reader had half copied the page entitled *Ode to a Nightingale*. He picked up the sheet and after studying the words for some moments, folded the paper and placed it in his inside coat pocket.

Ravenscroft looked at the walls of the room, but could find no pictures or framed photographs. There seemed little to show for a life of nearly thirty years. He searched in vain for a diary, or any other documents of a personal nature, and then walked over to the window, where he stood for some minutes looking out at the view across the driveway towards the abbey in the distance.

As he turned once more to face the interior of the room, he felt again its cold and loneliness. Why had this young woman lived and died here, in this room full of such sadness and such emptiness? It was as if the room's occupant had sought to eradicate all that had happened to her in the past, seeking no remembrance, whilst scarcely living in the present, but without any hope for the future. And yet there had been that poem, suggesting that its reader had perhaps glimpsed the unattainable, however briefly for a moment in time.

Ravenscroft's thoughts were suddenly disturbed by the opening of the door.

'I've left the maid with Talbot and his wife,' said Crabb entering the room.

'How did they seem when you broke the news to them?'

'I thought Talbot was going to collapse, and his wife was speechless for once. Did you find anything in the room, sir?'

'There are no personal diaries, letters, photographs or anything else of that sort. She seems to have been quite alone in the world. I did find this though,' said Ravenscroft reaching into his pocket and handing the sheet of blue paper to Crabb.

'Seems to be a poem of some sort,' said Crabb after reading the lines to himself.

'*Ode to a Nightingale* by Keats. The poem is not important, but the handwriting is. Compare it with the letter that was sent to me,' said Ravenscroft passing over the other sheet.

'Seems remarkably like the same hand.'

'Exactly my thoughts, Tom.'

'So it was Miss Martin who sent you the letter telling us that the poison had been placed in Jones's port bottle,' said Crabb handing back the sheets to Ravenscroft.

'It would appear so, which means that if she knew how Jones met his death, she must also have known who committed the crime — '

'And that was why she had to be poisoned — '

'Before she could tell us. If only she had spoken out when we first interviewed her, all this could have been avoided. Now the poor woman is dead, and we now have two murders on our hands. What on earth possessed her to remain silent?'

'Perhaps there were two of them in it, and

she didn't want to betray the other one?' suggested Crabb.

'A lover of some kind perhaps? That would suggest Talbot, I suppose — but if that was the case, why did she then send us that letter? After all we had all but given up the case until that letter arrived. Why write such a letter? She must have known that we would return here once we received it — and yet she was very much on her guard when we questioned her, giving nothing away. A strange business, unless — yes, of course, how stupid we have been! She was blackmailing the murderer!' exclaimed Ravenscroft.

'I don't understand, sir,' said Crabb.

'Don't you see, Tom, she knew who had poisoned Jones, and was hoping to receive some kind of payment, or favour, in return for keeping silent.'

'I see that, but why then send us the letter?'

'Because she wanted us to return and question the murderer further, thereby putting a greater value on her own silence.'

'Very clever.'

'Yes, but of course, the murderer decided to poison her rather than pay her for her silence. She must have thought that the killer would have paid her, believing that she was safe whilst she knew the truth. The killer of course thought otherwise, and decided to remove her before she could talk. The poor woman, she had so little, and must have seen that this was her one opportunity to escape from this dreadful place. If only she had told us, Tom, if only,' said an annoyed Ravenscroft pacing up and down the room.

'Terrible way to go,' muttered Crabb. 'She must have died quite quickly.'

'The question we have to answer now, Tom, is who killed her? Someone in this house poisoned Jones, for some unknown reason, then decided to silence Miss Martin.'

'Well I believe that Talbot is our killer,' suggested Crabb.

'Oh, why do you say that?'

'Well it seems likely that the two of them had some kind of relationship, and that would explain why she didn't come straight out with it that Talbot was our man. Then as you say, she told him that she had seen him put poison in the bottle of port, and promised to keep quiet in return for either money or personal favours,' continued Crabb.

'I must say I am inclined to agree with you. Talbot is our most likely suspect at this stage in our inquiries. I can't see either Turco, or Jacobson, in a relationship with Miss Martin. I suppose there is Cherrington. He would certainly charm the young lady — and of course we have yet to meet the mysterious

Claybourne,' replied Ravenscroft deep in thought for some moments. 'No, you are right, Tom. Let's go and confront Talbot. He should be able to tell us more, and I don't believe that he threw away all of Jones's possessions either.'

★ ★ ★

'Well, Talbot, this is a bad business,' said Ravenscroft as he sat facing the landlord and his wife across the table in the dining room at Talbots'.

'Poor Miss Martin. Who can have done such a thing?' muttered the ashen-faced Talbot.

'Who indeed? I am hoping that you may be able to cast some light on this matter.'

'We will do all we can,' said Mrs Talbot.

'What can you tell me about Miss Martin? Did she ever mention any friends or relatives? We will need to inform them of her demise,' asked Ravenscroft intently.

'She never mentioned any relatives to us,' answered Talbot.

'Never had any visitors neither,' added his wife.

'Did she ever receive any letters or any other form of communication?'

'No. Never ever saw any letters.'

'So you are telling me that she was all alone

in the world, without friends or acquaintances?'

'That's how it was,' said Mrs Talbot.

'Strange, but then again I suppose some people do go through their whole lives without forming any close friendships. What was your relationship with the dead woman?' asked Ravenscroft leaning forwards across the table, and staring directly at the landlord, over the top of his spectacles.

'What relationship? I don't know what you are talking about,' replied Talbot defensively.

'Oh, come now, Talbot, we know you and Miss Martin were quite close.'

'Who says so?'

'Your wife has indicated as such,' continued Ravenscroft.

'Just gossip. It was nothing,'

'Look, Talbot, either you tell me now the full details of your relationship with your lodger, or you can accompany both of us to the station and we will continue with our questions there,' said Ravenscroft becoming annoyed with his suspect.

'He was infatuated with her,' sneered Mrs Talbot. 'You was always making some excuse to go up to her room. You think I don't know what was going on between you two?'

'Be quiet, woman! You don't know what you're talking about,' retaliated Talbot.

'I knows what you were up to. You can't fool me. Think I'm daft?'

'I never did anything. I was sorry for her. All alone in the world. It was all quite innocent. That's all there was to it.'

Ravenscroft sat back his chair, realizing that if he remained quiet, and let the landlord and his wife argue against each other, then it was possible that the truth would eventually be forthcoming.

'Lies, Talbot, lies! All of it lies. I've seen the way you looked at her,' scowled Mrs Talbot.

'I tells you, woman, there was nothing to it.'

'The way you were always asking if she wanted anything.'

'I was only being considerate.'

'Considerate! You don't know the meaning of the word!'

'Why is it that you always sees the worst in me?'

''Cause that's what you are like, you miserable little worm of a man. I wouldn't mind so much, if she was the first, but no, there were others,' sneered the landlady.

'What others?'

'Oh, you've forgotten Miss Clements. She only stayed a month and couldn't leave soon enough. You were all over her like a cold stinging nettle.'

'I never laid a finger on her, Letitia,'

'Then there was Miss Milson, she left after the first week.'

'That was ten years ago.'

'Why you can't leave these women alone, I'll never know.'

'I think perhaps this is getting us nowhere,' interjected Ravenscroft. 'Now Talbot, were you, or were you not, having an improper relationship with Miss Martin?'

'No, I was not! And any of them that says I was, is telling lies,' protested the landlord looking directly across the room to where his wife stood.

'So I'm the liar now, am I?'

'Please, Mrs Talbot, can we have an end to this? Did you and Miss Martin poison Jones?' asked Ravenscroft addressing Talbot once more.

'Of course we didn't. Why would we want to kill Jones?'

'For his valuables,' suggested Crabb who had been standing by the door making notes in his pocketbook.

'What valuables? I've told you, there was no valuables.'

'Oh yes, you mentioned that when you cleaned out the room, there was nothing there of a personal nature. Well I have to tell you that I don't believe you. I think the dead man did have something of worth, and I think you took it for yourself,' said Ravenscroft leaning forwards once more and confronting the landlord directly.

'I've told you there was nothing there,' protested Talbot.

'May I remind you that it is a criminal offence to withhold vital evidence in respect of an investigation. If ever we are to find out why your lodger was poisoned I need those items. Now you have two choices — either you tell me what you took from the dead man's room, and produce the items for us now, or I'll take you away to the cells for the night, while my men take this house apart, inch by inch, until we find what we are looking for. Which is it to be, Talbot?' said Ravenscroft becoming more and more annoyed.

'For goodness sake Talbot, tell them. If you don't, I will,' said the landlady glaring at her husband.

'Well Talbot? What is it to be? I'm a busy man. I have not the time to sit here all day,' said Ravenscroft quickly rising to his feet.

'All right, all right!' shouted Talbot. 'I'll fetch them. They're hidden in the backyard. I don't want them anyway.'

'Crabb, go with him,' instructed Ravenscroft resuming his seat.

'After you, sir,' said Crabb opening the door.

A disgruntled Talbot led the way out of the room.

'The silly man. I told him all along that he should have handed the things in,' muttered the landlady.

'It would have been better if he had listened to you, Mrs Talbot.'

'What will happen to him now? He meant no harm by it. I knows he is a silly old cluttock, but he didn't kill neither Mr Jones nor Miss Martin. You has to believe that,' continued the woman.

Ravenscroft turned away and said nothing.

'Here they are,' said Talbot returning to the room and throwing an old bag onto the dining room table.

'Hidden under a pile of coal,' announced Crabb following on behind.

'Right. Let us see what we have here,' said Ravenscroft reaching into the bag, as the landlord resumed his seat. 'A silver pocket watch. Quite an expensive one by the face and decoration I would say. I wonder if there is an inscription inside? Yes, here we are. 'Charles Murphy. 1872.' That must be the man's real name. What is this wrapped up in this old towel?'

'Good lord!' exclaimed Crabb. 'It's a pistol.'

'And a very nasty one at that. Percussion

pocket pistol. Name of the maker on the side — 'John Elliott' that's all. Better see that it is unloaded. Yes. And this the box of bullets that go with. Was there anything else?'

'No. That's all there was,' replied a sullen Talbot.

'I don't believe you. Was there any money on the dead man?'

'No.'

'I tell you, I don't believe you,' said Ravenscroft raising his voice.

'For goodness sake, Talbot, why don't you tell him? There was two five pound notes in his inside pocket,' said the landlady.

'We will need those as well.'

Mrs Talbot rose from her chair, walked over to the side cabinet, opened the drawer, took out two notes and handed them over to Ravenscroft.

'Were there any papers on the deceased? Perhaps a wallet of some kind? This is vitally important; we need to find out all we can about this man,' said Ravenscroft accepting the notes, and realizing that there had probably been more.

'There was nothing. He had nothing else on him. I'm telling you the truth,' pleaded Talbot.

'Very well. That will be all for now,' said Ravenscroft wrapping the gun up in the towel and returning it to the bag.

'What will happen to Talbot now?' asked an anxious Mrs Talbot.

'Nothing for the present. You have been a very foolish man, Talbot. If you had told us all this at the beginning Miss Martin might still be alive today. Think yourself fortunate that you are not up before the bench tomorrow morning,' said Ravenscroft lifting up the bag and walking over towards the door. 'Tom, I want you to stay here until the men come from the mortuary. I'll take this back to the station. Good day to you, Talbot. Mrs Talbot.'

'You silly man,' chided the landlady glaring across at her husband.

Talbot looked sheepishly down at the floor as Ravenscroft left the room.

* * *

'Hoskings! Hoskings!' cried out Ravenscroft as he entered the police station.

'Inspector Ravenscroft,' replied the startled constable quickly emerging from the inner room, whilst trying to disguise a mouthful of sandwich.

'Hoskings, I want you to put this in the safe,' said Ravenscroft banging the bag down on the counter.

'What is it, sir?' asked the constable

145

swallowing quickly.

'A pistol and some other things belonging to the dead man Jones. Talbot had taken them and hidden them in the back yard.'

'Yes, sir. Right away, sir,' replied the policeman picking up the bag, whilst cramming the remains of his sandwich into his coat pocket.

'You've no doubt heard that Miss Martin has been poisoned?'

'Yes, sir.'

'Have you been eating whilst on duty, Hoskings?' asked a suspicious Ravenscroft.

'No, sir.'

'You know it is a police infringement to eat whilst on duty?'

'Of course, sir.'

'If I find that you have been eating it will be the worst for you. Do you understand, Hoskings?'

'Yes, sir,' said the constable becoming red in the face.

'Now, when you have locked that away, I want you to tell me how many chemists there are in Pershore.'

'Yes, sir,' said the policeman disappearing from view with the bag in his hand.

Ravenscroft remained deep in thought, drumming his fingers impatiently on the counter top until the other returned.

'Well, Hoskings?'

'What, sir?'

'How many chemists are there here in Pershore?' asked an annoyed Ravenscroft.

'Chemists? Chemists?'

'Yes, chemists, man. How many are there?'

'Just the two, sir.'

'Yes, and they are?'

'Brights in the market place and Ollenshaws at the bottom of the road, sir.'

'Right,' said Ravenscroft turning to leave the room.

'What do you want me to do, sir?' asked the constable.

'Nothing for the present, Hoskings. You can stay here.'

'Yes, sir.'

'And Hoskings?'

'Yes, sir?'

'Make sure you don't eat whilst on duty.'

'Yes sir.'

★　★　★

Ravenscroft pushed open the door of the chemist's shop and found himself in a small dingy room, three sides of which were covered with tall shelves containing various bottles of coloured liquid and other medical preparations. An elderly, grey-haired man

147

stood behind the counter busily engaged in writing in a large ledger, whilst humming a tune to himself.

Ravenscroft coughed.

The man continued with his activities.

'Have I the honour of addressing Mr Ollenshaw?' asked Ravenscroft walking up to the counter.

'One moment, sir. Twenty six shillings and five pence . . . hum, hum . . . two shillings and three pence halfpenny . . . hum, hum . . . no, that won't do at all . . . hum, hum . . . three shillings and one farthing . . . hum, hum . . . one shilling and two pence . . . hum, hum . . . yes, that's better . . . hum, hum . . . now let us see . . . hum, hum . . . next week . . . hum, hum . . . hum, hum . . . '

'Are you Mr Ollenshaw, or not?' interrupted Ravenscroft becoming annoyed by the long wait and the man's musical interludes.

The man looked up at Ravenscroft. 'In a hurry are we?'

'As a matter of fact, I am.'

'One moment, sir . . . hum, hum . . . ' said the man looking down at the ledger once more.

'Look here, are you the owner of this establishment or not?' asked Ravenscroft, realizing that he was raising his voice.

'Yes, sir . . . hum, hum . . . three shillings

and sixpence . . . '

'My name is Ravenscroft, Inspector Ravenscroft. I have come on a matter of great urgency.'

'Ah, sir,' replied the man suddenly closing his ledger with a bang so that particles of dust drifted upwards into the air. 'Police. You should have said so earlier.'

'So you are Ollenshaw?' asked Ravenscroft.

'Snook. Simeon Snook. Ollenshaw is dead . . . hum, hum . . . '

'I'm sorry to hear that.'

'Are you? I'm not. He ran off with all the money twenty-seven years ago, leaving me to run the establishment on my own . . . hum, hum.'

'Then how do you know he is dead, if he ran away all those years ago?' enquired Ravenscroft regretting that he had asked the question as soon as he had asked it.

'Because he was eighty years of age at the time, and if he were still alive now he would be a hundred and five, hum, hum.'

'A hundred and seven, surely,' corrected Ravenscroft.

'Hum, are you doubting my word, sir?' stared the chemist.

'Eighty and twenty-seven makes one hundred and seven, not one hundred and five, but never mind that. I am making inquiries about your supplies of arsenic.'

'Arsenic? Then you will also be making inquiries about that lodger who died at Talbots'?'

'That is correct. I see that news travels fast.'

'This is a small town, sir. Nothing remains hidden for long,' said the man attempting a fleeting grimace.

'Then you will no doubt have heard that there has been a further poisoning at Talbots'?'

'One of the other lodgers? Hum, hum.'

'I would like to know whether anyone from Talbots' has been here recently purchasing arsenic from you?' asked Ravenscroft.

'Hum, hum,' replied Snook looking up at the ceiling, his head on one side and appearing to be deep in thought.

'Well?' asked an annoyed Ravenscroft after some moments had elapsed. 'I would not have thought it was a difficult question to answer.'

'Would you not, sir? Hum, hum. The Miss Fanshaws are customers.'

'Really,' said an intrigued Ravenscroft. 'Are they regular customers of yours?'

'Indeed sir.'

'And have they purchased any arsenic from you recently?'

'Liver pills and water for the complexion . . . hum, hum.'

'Is that all the ladies purchased?'

'Yes. Hum, hum, hum, hum,' said the man beginning to move away.

'I would like to inspect your Poisons Register, if I may,' said Ravenscroft.

'Poisons Register, you say? We keep such a book of course, but it is not open to anyone to inspect, hum, hum.'

'May I remind you, Mr Snook, that I am a police officer, and that I am investigating the deaths of two people in this town, whom I believe were poisoned with arsenic. As their murderer procured arsenic from somewhere, it must be a strong possibility that it could have been purchased from here. Now sir, the Poisons Register if you please.'

Snook disappeared from view into the back room, and returned shortly bearing another ledger, which he placed on the counter.

'Thank you,' said Ravenscroft opening the book.

'Everyone who requests arsenic and other poisons is included. You will find no irregularities at Ollenshaws,' said Snook peering over his spectacles.

Ravenscroft ran his fingers over the entries for the past six months of the register as the chemist returned to the back room humming a tune to himself.

'Well I declare!' exclaimed Ravenscroft

151

closing the book with a bang.

'Found what we are looking for, sir?' asked Snook peering round the door frame.

'Indeed I have. Yes, certainly. Thank you for your assistance, Mr Snook. Good day to you, sir.'

7

Pershore

'Well, Mrs Jacobson, perhaps you would care to tell Constable Crabb and myself why you purchased a quantity of arsenic powder last week from Ollenshaws the chemists?'

Ravenscroft and Crabb faced the young woman across the table in Talbot's living room.

'I have a perfectly plausible explanation for purchasing the powder, inspector. It is for my complexion,' replied Mrs Jacobson somewhat nervously, avoiding the detective's gaze.

'Perhaps you would care to elaborate?' suggested Ravenscroft.

'I have rather a dark, unclear complexion. I find that if I mix a little of the arsenic with some vinegar and chalk, and then apply the mixture to my face it not only improves my complexion, but also hides any imperfections.'

'I see,' replied Ravenscroft somewhat taken aback by the matter of fact explanation.

'It is not uncommon for ladies with similar problems to indulge in this practice.'

'But perhaps a little unwise knowing the nature of the arsenic?' added Ravenscroft, not entirely convinced by the young woman's story.

'I am careful to only use a little, of course,' said Mrs Jacobson forcing a brief smile.

'I must also tell you, ma'am, that I inspected the Poisons Register at Ollenshaws for the past six months and could find no further entries in your name.'

'That is indeed true. As I said, Mr Ravenscroft, I only use a small amount of the arsenic in the mixture. It lasts a long time. It must be a year, or more, since my previous purchase.'

'So if I look back further in the register I would find your name again?' asked a suspicious Ravenscroft.

'I cannot remember exactly when, and where I purchased the previous amount.'

'I must say, Mrs Jacobson, that I find all this difficult to accept. Two people have died from poisoning in this establishment, within a few days of each other, and I have discovered that you purchased a quantity of arsenic from a local chemist only a few days before all this happened. Rather a coincidence, would you not agree?' suggested Ravenscroft.

'I have told you the truth, inspector. What else can I tell you?'

'Is your husband aware that you use arsenic in your facial preparations?'

'I would not have thought so,' smiled Mrs Jacobson. 'What a lady does in her dressing room is her concern, as I am sure that your wife would tell you. Anyway my husband is quite blind, as I know you are aware.'

Ravenscroft sat back in his chair. He had entered the room a few minutes previous thoroughly expecting to elicit a confession from the murderer of Jones and Miss Martin, but now realizing that perhaps his optimism had been somewhat premature and that he would now have to change his line of questioning.

'You mentioned that you met your husband in London, five years ago?'

'That is correct. I know that many people find it difficult to accept that we are married given the difference in our ages, but I can assure you, inspector, that my husband and I are perfectly happy together.'

'You met in Whitechapel?'

'Yes, my husband informed you of that fact. We were staying at the same lodging house.'

'Ah yes, the Crosskeys.'

'That is so,' replied Mrs Jacobson moving uneasily in her seat.

'You might be interested to know that I

155

used to be a police officer in the Whitechapel District, before my arrival in Ledbury. I know the Crosskeys quite well. It is not the kind of establishment that young respectable ladies frequent,' said Ravenscroft studying the woman's face intently.

'I think you are mistaken. I would not have stayed in a boarding house or similar establishment that was not beyond reproach. I may have been only a simple seamstress, but nevertheless I had a reputation to uphold, as I am sure you would appreciate.'

'So you were not aware of the reputation of the Crosskeys as the kind of establishment frequented by certain *ladies of the night*?'

'No. I was not there for very long, and must admit that I was not fully aware of the nature of the lives my fellow lodgers lived. I worked quite long hours in one of the nearby factories and came home to the Crosskeys late at night.'

'And where did you live before your arrival at Crosskeys?' asked Ravenscroft, not fully accepting this explanation.

'I lived in a small village in Essex. I left there and came to London looking for work.'

'Thank you, Mrs Jacobson. I think that will be all for now,' said Ravenscroft bringing the interview to an abrupt end, much to Crabb's surprise.

156

'What I have told you, inspector, is the truth. I did not poison either Mr Jones or Miss Martin. I would have no reason to do so,' said Mrs Jacobson rising from her chair.

'Nevertheless we will need to question you further as our investigation progresses. Do you still have the arsenic?' asked Ravenscroft as Crabb moved to open the door.

'Yes.'

'Then I think it would be better if we were to take possession of it.'

'Yes, if you insist?'

'I do, Mrs Jacobson. I do.'

'Then I will fetch it for you.'

Crabb closed the door as the woman left the room. 'You let her off lightly, sir.'

'There was little to be gained by continuing to question her further at this stage.'

'I don't believe all that story about mixing up the arsenic and plastering it all over her face,' continued Crabb.

'Oh Tom, women will do all sorts of peculiar things to improve their looks,' smiled Ravenscroft.

'Not that old Jacobson would know.'

'That is so, but there may be someone else who appreciates her efforts. You may recall that when we were making our way here earlier today we observed Mrs Jacobson busily walking down the road, as if she were hurrying to meet someone.'

'You think she has a secret admirer?'

'Who knows, Tom?'

The door opened and Mrs Jacobson entered the room once more.

'There you are, inspector. Here is the arsenic.'

'Thank you, Mrs Jacobson,' said Ravenscroft taking possession of the substance.

'I would appreciate it, inspector, if you were not to mention this matter to my husband.'

'I am afraid I cannot give you that guarantee. If we find as our investigations proceed that we need to inform your husband of our concerns, then so be it.'

Mrs Jacobson said nothing as she left the room.

'It would appear that a quantity of the arsenic has been used, but of course we don't know how much of it she has used for her beauty preparation, or if any was used to poison Jones and Miss Martin. She may be telling us the truth. One thing that has been concerning me about this case — were both victims poisoned with arsenic, or was some other poison used?'

'Oh, why do you ask that, sir?' asked Crabb.

'I have always believed that death from

arsenic poisoning could take a long time. Those who have died so usually complain of feeling unwell over a number of days, or even weeks, before they receive the last, final fatal dose that kills them. If we assume that both Jones and Miss Martin do not fall into that category, then they would have had to consume quite a large dose on the nights they were killed. Also if arsenic were used, the murderer could not have been sure that his victims had drunk enough of it to have brought about their ends.'

'Yes, sir, but perhaps someone might have been putting smaller doses of the arsenic in Jones's port each night, leading up to the larger, fatal dose?' suggested Crabb.

'Yes, but somehow I don't think so. If that had been the case, Jones would have been ill for some days before his death, and yet no one has remarked that that was the case. No, I think that some other poison was used, a poison that would be sure to kill its victim after drinking only one small, but lethal, dose.'

'That rather lets Mrs Jacobson off our lists of suspects.'

'Perhaps. We must keep an open mind. Whether it was arsenic, or some other poison, our murderer may well have purchased the poison in some other town, many miles from here, even using a false name so that they would never be traced. If that is the case, then it is going to make our task even more difficult.'

'What do we do next, sir?' asked Crabb.

'I believe that we should certainly keep Mrs Jacobson under close observation. I would be interested to know whether she is in the habit of leaving the house on her own, and if so, how often she does so. If that is the case then I would like to know where she goes to, and whom she meets.'

'The maid should be able to answer your first question, sir.'

'Good thinking, Tom. Let us go into the kitchen. We may find her there.'

*   *   *

'Yes sir, Mrs Jacobson often leaves the house on her own,' said Maisie drying her hands on a towel at the side of the sink.

'How often does she do this?' asked Ravenscroft.

'Two or three times a week, sir, I would say.'

'And how long is she away?'

'An hour or so, I would think, sir. Always in the early afternoon.'

'That is interesting. I don't suppose you

would happen to know where she goes to, would you?'

'No sir. I'm afraid I can't help you.'

'On the contrary, Maisie, you have been most informative. There is something you could do for us, however.'

'Yes sir, anything, of course,' said the maid eagerly.

'Next time you observe that Mrs Jacobson has left the house, I would be obliged that you would inform us as soon as she has left the building, providing of course that either Constable Crabb or myself are here at the time. Do you understand?'

'Yes sir — and if you are not here?'

'Then make a note of the time the lady leaves, and when she returns.'

'Yes, sir. Oh, you don't think that Mrs Jacobson poisoned Mr Jones and poor Miss Martin? How awful,' said the maid becoming agitated.

'No, we don't know that at all, Maisie. We would just like to be aware of everyone's whereabouts.'

'Yes, sir. I will do my best.'

'I'm sure you will. There is one other thing that you can help us with.'

'Yes, sir, anything.'

'I don't suppose Mr Claybourne has returned yet?'

'No, sir.'

'Do you know when he is likely to return?'

'No, sir. He just comes and goes when he wants to.'

'Then I would like to see his room. Have you got a key?'

'Mr Claybourne has one, and we have a set of duplicate keys to all the rooms,' replied the maid.

'And where are these keys kept?' asked Ravenscroft.

'They are all on a ring, which we hang up there by the door.'

'I see. Then anyone can have access to another person's room if they take those keys?'

'Yes, I suppose so.'

'I wonder if you could possibly unlock Mr Claybourne's room for us,' smiled Ravenscroft.

'I'm not sure that is allowed, sir.'

'I admire your caution and vigilance, Maisie, but two people have died already in this house, and if we are to apprehend the culprit, it is important that we follow all lines of enquiry.'

'Mrs Talbot won't like it, sir, if she finds out.'

'Then we shall not tell her. Where is Mrs Talbot at present?'

'Visiting some friends, sir. She won't be back until six.'

'Then there is no time like the present.'

The maid took down the set of keys and led the way up the steps to the first landing.

'This is Mr Claybourne's room, sir,' she said taking one of the keys and turning it in the lock.

'Thank you, Maisie. I think we can manage now, thank you,' said Ravenscroft opening the door.

'Yes sir,' replied the maid turning away and beginning her descent down the stairs.

Ravenscroft and Crabb stepped into the room.

'It looks as though there is just one room here. Claybourne obviously sleeps over there. Otherwise just a table, chair, small wardrobe and washstand. Not much in the way of creature comforts, but if he is seldom here so I presume he does not require much. Have a look in the wardrobe, while I go through these papers on the table,' said Ravenscroft picking up the collection of documents.

'Nothing in the wardrobe, sir, only a shirt, spare pair of trousers and a few other garments,' said Crabb presently.

'This is interesting, Tom. I think I have discovered what our mysterious Mr Claybourne does for a living. He is an insurance agent with The London, Liverpool and Globe Insurance Company. I suppose that would explain why he is only here for a day or so at a time. He must spend the rest of his time either visiting other parts of the country, or taking his policies to the head office in London,' said Ravenscroft continuing to thumb through the pile of papers.

'Interesting,' remarked Crabb. 'Perhaps he insured Jones and Miss Martin?'

'I don't think so. As both of them appear to have led solitary single lives there would have been no beneficiaries, so I don't think we can say Claybourne, or anyone else, murdered them for the insurance money. Ah, this is interesting. Take a look at this, Tom.'

Ravenscroft passed over one of the documents to his assistant.

'Professor Jacobson's name is at the top,' said Crabb.

'Yes a life policy for three hundred pounds taken out on the life of Professor Jacobson, the main beneficiary to be his wife Mrs Rosana Jacobson.'

'I am surprised he got cover given his age,' remarked Crabb.

'Yes, that is surprising. Perhaps Claybourne was so anxious to sign him up that he was not too fussy about the details. See when the policy was taken out Tom.'

'Three months ago,' said Crabb after studying the paper.

'Three months ago,' repeated Ravenscroft. 'And Mrs Jacobson has just purchased some arsenic!'

'You don't think she bought the arsenic with the intention of poisoning her husband, so that she could claim the insurance money?'

'If that was her intention, then it is a good thing we have taken the arsenic away from her. Of course, she wouldn't be the first wife to kill her husband for insurance money. Alternatively, she may have been telling us the truth when she said that she only required the arsenic for her beauty preparation. I suppose there is no way of telling.'

'Shouldn't we warn Jacobson?' suggested Crabb.

'Not just yet. I think she would only deny any accusations. We would need to secure further evidence against her before we could proceed in that direction. All the more important to know where she goes when she leaves the house. She could be meeting an admirer, and the two of them could have been planning the old man's demise, but all this is pure speculation.'

'Perhaps her admirer is Claybourne?'

'That's an idea. Another possibility, but only a speculative one at present, is that

Claybourne persuaded the old man to insure his life, leaving the money to Mrs Jacobson on his death. In the meantime Claybourne does not appear to have insured anyone else here at Talbots', and as far as I can ascertain these remaining policies appear to be in order. We will just have to wait for Claybourne's return then we can question him further, and confront him and Mrs Jacobson together,' said Ravenscroft returning the papers to the table.

'What shall we do next, sir?' asked Crabb.

'It is late today, Tom, and we have not eaten. Time we returned home to partake of some refreshment and gather our thoughts in preparation for tomorrow.'

8

Ledbury

Ravenscroft retired late, and after changing his position a number of times from one side of the bed to the other, much to his wife's annoyance, fell into a fitful sleep, where the events of the previous few days each sought prominence against each other. The faces of the Talbots, the professor and his wife, the Fanshaw sisters, Turco and Cherrington, each came into view seeking to eclipse one another.

Then again Ravenscroft found himself in the dead woman's bedroom staring down at the corpse, before the scene was replaced by a greasy Talbot waving a pistol round above his head in the kitchen of the lodging house, and then to the chemist's shop where the large coloured bottles tumbled down, one after another, onto the top of his head. Then he saw himself running up and down the creaking flights of stairs, in pursuit of a dark, mysterious, laughing figure, whom he could never quite reach, and who gradually receded into the distance — and all the time there was

167

the wild music of Turco's violin in the background, coupled with the laughter of a grinning Cherrington.

'It's Cherrington!' exclaimed Ravenscroft suddenly waking up in a cold sweat and sitting bolt upright in bed.

'Whatever is the matter, Samuel?' groaned a half-conscious Lucy.

'It's Cherrington. He is the Pimlico poisoner!'

'I thought you were investigating a crime in Pershore, not Pimlico?'

'Yes, but Cherrington was the Pimlico poisoner. I knew I had seen him somewhere before!'

'Can't this wait until the morning, Samuel,' said Lucy turning over on her side.

'Yes, of course. I'm sorry. How silly of me not to have recognized him, after all these years. It's Quinton again.'

'Samuel!' sighed Lucy drawing the bed-clothes over her head.

'Yes, sorry my dear,' said Ravenscroft lying down once more.

★ ★ ★

'So you think it was Mr Cherrington who poisoned Jones and Miss Martin?' asked Lucy pouring out the tea at the breakfast

168

table. 'I thought you said yesterday that it was probably Mrs Jacobson who had killed them?'

'Well yes, I still believe that the Jew's wife is our most likely suspect, but this morning I am not quite so sure,' replied Ravenscroft vigorously buttering a slice of toast.

'You were talking about Pimlico. What has that to do with the murders in Pershore?'

'Ah well — perhaps I had better start at the beginning.'

'I think that would be a good idea.'

'Well, many years ago, when I first joined the police force in London, I was sent to the local police station in Pimlico, just north of the river, where my superior officer was an inspector in late middle-age by the name of Robertson. I remember he was always coughing and sneezing as though he had some dreadful cold, which he could never throw off, but that is by the by. Robertson was one of the old band of policemen, not quite old enough to have been one of the original Runners or Peelers, but not far off. He was very strict with us young constables and came down hard on any criminals who came his way, and he often boasted that he always caught his man. Anyway after I had been there for a few months, one afternoon Robertson and I were called to a house in Pimlico where the wife of a certain Captain

Quinton had just suddenly died. She had apparently been ill with stomach ailments for two or three weeks, and the couple had only been married for a month or so.'

'How sad,' interjected Lucy.

'Yes, she was quite young, in her mid-twenties I would say. Anyway, Robertson suspected that she had probably died as the result of arsenic poisoning, and suspicion naturally fell on her new husband, especially when we learned that she had brought a sizeable settlement with her to the marriage.'

'You think he married her for her money?'

'That seemed most likely, but the thing which damned Quinton was that we found a diary which the young lady had kept both before and after her marriage. In this diary she recounted how she had come to Pershore to recover from the loss of her betrothed who had been killed in India, and how she met her future husband there.'

'Ah, I see where Pershore fits into the narrative,' said Lucy after sipping her tea.

'Quite. What was interesting, however was the last entry in the diary, which was scarcely legible, but which quite plainly implicated her husband, in that she claimed that he was poisoning her.'

'The awful man! He should have hung.'

'Yes, he deserved to, the evidence was plain

for all to see, and the case came quickly to trial, but poor Robertson had not reckoned on Sefton Rawlinson.'

'Whoever was Sefton Rawlinson?'

'Sefton Rawlinson was, and is, the most underhand, craftiest, slippery brief in the whole of the Old Bailey.'

'Sounds as though you don't like him?'

'I do not indeed. I have brought many criminals to court over the years only to find that they have escaped justice on some technicality, or fabrication, offered to the jury by Sefton Rawlinson. But to go back to the *Pimlico Poisoning* case as the newspapers called it, Rawlinson claimed that the last diary entries had been written by a deranged woman, who was so ill and delirious at the time of writing, that she was under the mistaken impression that her husband was responsible for her illness. The jury believed this nonsense of course, and when Rawlinson called Quinton, he presented himself as the distraught loving husband, whose life had been blighted by the sad demise of the woman he had loved. The prosecution could bring no evidence to prove that Quinton had actually murdered his wife, and as arsenic leaves neither smell nor taste, he was quickly acquitted. Poor old Robertson never got over the case. He had always firmly believed that

Quinton had been guilty of the crime, and he left the force shortly afterwards, an embittered man, and somewhat under a cloud. Within a few weeks I was also sent off to Whitechapel, a far different area from peaceful, relatively genteel Pimlico.'

'So this Captain Quinton went free?' asked Lucy intrigued by the narrative.

'Yes, unfortunately. There was nothing we could do about it, until now.'

'So you believe that your Mr Cherrington is none other than this Captain Quinton?'

'I am sure of it. As soon as I saw him I had the strong impression that I'd seen him somewhere before. Of course it has been over twenty years since the *Pimlico Poisoning* case, and Quinton was probably in his late twenties then, clean shaven, but still with the same haughty, over confident manner. Now he has a moustache and beard, and is much older, but I am convinced he is the same man. Strange that he has returned to the same town where he met his wife. He must be on the lookout for another young woman to marry,' said Ravenscroft eating a piece of toast.

'How dreadful. So if this Quinton poisoned his first wife, he most likely poisoned Jones and Miss Martin as well?'

'That would seem most likely, but why? I

don't really understand, but yes that is it. He must have been courting Miss Martin with the intention of making her his next wife and thereby acquiring her fortune.'

'But why would he have poisoned her before he married her — and anyway you said that this Miss Martin appeared to have lived a meagre existence.'

'That is not to say that she did not have money elsewhere, or perhaps she was to inherit money upon her marriage, and Quinton found out about this and saw her as his next victim,' suggested Ravenscroft.

'But if that had been the case why would he have first felt the need to poison Jones?'

'Perhaps Jones and Cherrington had met somewhere in the past, and Jones rather than speak out decided to blackmail him. Cherrington then decided to poison Jones to get him out of the way, and so that he could continue to woo Miss Martin.'

'Yes, but if that was so, why did he then kill Miss Martin before he had chance to marry her?'

'Maybe she found out that Cherrington had poisoned Jones, so he was left with no other choice than to poison her as well.'

'The dreadful man! You must bring him to book, Samuel.'

'Easier said than done. We have to

remember that we are dealing with a very clever, cunning man, and that he was acquitted by a jury. We also have no evidence that he poisoned either Miss Martin or Jones. Unless I can find the arsenic on him and break him down with our questions, there may not be much chance of arresting him, but I tell you, Lucy, I intend to have a very good go. He will not escape the law this time. But enough of all this. You have decided to go to Weymouth later this morning?'

'I think I should wait a day or two until this case is over. I'd so like you to come as well,' said Lucy smiling.

'And I should like to accompany you and the boys. No, I think you should definitely go this morning. After all you have made the reservations and Susan will be going with you to take care of little Arthur. I will follow on in a day or so, later in the week I promise, as soon as I have extracted a confession from Cherrington. There will still be a few days we can share together.'

'No, I am quite happy to wait, at least until tomorrow,' offered Lucy.

'No, I will not hear of it. You will go. I insist upon it.'

'Very well, if you are sure that you can take care of yourself whilst we are away?'

'Lucy, my dear, I was used to looking after

myself for forty years before I met you, so I am sure that I will not starve for a day or so, and there is always the local inns if I do get desperate. I shall miss you all horribly, but I know that a week in Weymouth will be of great benefit to you all. So there is an end to the matter. What time does your train depart?'

★ ★ ★

'An interesting account, sir,' said Crabb cracking the whip as the trap made its way along the winding back lane that led into the town later that morning.

'Yes, Cherrington, or Quinton, to give him his proper name, has been quite devious, but this time I mean to bring him to account for all his crimes,' replied a determined Ravenscroft.

'I wonder how many other poor women he has trapped and married over the years?'

'Who knows, but I intend to find out. I don't believe for one minute all that nonsense he gave us about tea plantations in India, and smoking cigarettes with Turkish gentlemen on boats on the way home. Waiting for funds to arrive indeed.'

'Mrs Ravenscroft managed to catch the train then, sir?' asked Crabb changing the subject.

'Yes, thank you, Tom. I must say I am

rather envious of them.'

'Never mind, sir. We will soon have this Cherrington under lock and key.'

'I hope so, Tom. I hope so.'

Crabb brought the horse to a standstill at the end of the driveway, and he and Ravenscroft made their way towards the front door, just as a familiar figure was leaving the property.

'Ah, Mr Cherrington, we were just on our way to have a few words with you,' said Ravenscroft.

'Can't wait, I'm afraid. Have just heard that my funds might have arrived. On my way to the bank to verify the news. Have to leave your questions until later. Sorry, but I am sure you understand?' replied a breezy Cherrington, about to walk away.

'I'm afraid it can't wait, Mr Cherrington. I must insist that we have a few words with you now. It is most urgent,' said Ravenscroft firmly.

'Well, I don't know, this is most annoying,' complained Cherrington.

'You could always accompany us to the police station of course, and we could continue the conversation there,' suggested Ravenscroft.

'Look, no need for that, Ravenscroft. No need at all. I suppose I can put off the bank.

After four weeks of waiting for my money to arrive, I don't suppose another few minutes will cause any delay.'

'Thank you, Mr Cherrington. Perhaps if we could speak with you in the privacy of your own room?'

'Must be serious then. Yes, if you would care to follow me, gentlemen,' said Cherrington opening the door to the lodging house.

Ravenscroft and Crabb followed their suspect up the two flights of stairs and onto the upper landing, where Cherrington unlocked the door to his rooms.

'Can I offer you two gentlemen a drink or a cigarette?' offered their host, as Ravenscroft and Crabb seated themselves in the living room.

'No thank you, sir,' replied Ravenscroft, as Crabb took out his pocketbook.

'I hope you don't mind if I do?' asked Cherrington lighting a cigarette before sitting on the armchair before the burnt out remains of the previous night's fire.

'We have come about Miss Martin,' began Ravenscroft.

'Terrible business. The poor woman. I say, I hope you don't think I had anything to do with her death, do you? I hardly knew the woman.'

'I do not think that is quite the case, Mr

Cherrington. In fact I think you knew Miss Martin quite well.'

'I don't quite know where you get that idea from,' protested Cherrington leaning back in his chair and blowing smoke out into the room.

'I think you were going to marry her, to acquire her money,' said Ravenscroft coming quickly to the matter in hand.

'That is an absurd idea,' laughed Cherrington. 'Quite absurd. The woman had no attraction for me at all, and anyway she was apparently as poor as a church mouse.'

'Oh, how did you know that, Mr Cherrington?'

'It was obvious she had no money, otherwise she would not have been residing in this miserable little place. I find the suggestion that Miss Martin and I were in anyway attached to be quite ridiculous.'

'It is not so ridiculous as it sounds, Captain Quinton,' said Ravenscroft emphasizing the last two words as he leaned forwards.

'I'm sorry, I don't understand,' said Cherrington with a look of bewilderment.

'You don't remember the *Pimlico Poisoning* case then?' asked Ravenscroft studying his suspect intently over the top of his spectacles.

'What on earth was that?' laughed Cherrington.

'A young woman who was cruelly poisoned

over twenty years ago. I was there, Captain Quinton. I interviewed you and brought you to court,' said Ravenscroft anxious to press home his advantage.

'Look, what on earth are you talking about man? What on earth was this *Paddington Poisoning* case?'

'Pimlico, Mr Cherrington, Pimlico not Paddington,'

'Wherever it was then,' replied Cherrington showing slight signs of annoyance.

'You don't remember, Captain Quinton, how Inspector Robertson and a young constable interviewed you after the poisoning of the young woman?'

'Of course I don't. I've never heard of the *Pimlico Poisoning* case, or this Robertson person, or indeed this Quinton fellow. Quite clearly you are confusing me with someone else, inspector. You say all this was over twenty years ago? Clearly your memory is at fault, Ravenscroft, after all this length of time,' said Cherrington before inhaling deeply on his cigarette.

'Very clever, Mr Cherrington, but it will not do. I remember the case as though it were yesterday. You may have changed your appearance since then, but I still recognized you, Captain Quinton,' persisted Ravenscroft feeling slightly uneasy that he was in danger of losing his earlier advantage.

'Look, Ravenscroft, you have got all this horribly wrong. I am certainly not this Quinton that you seem to insist I am. I have never been to Pimlico in my life, and I have certainly never poisoned anyone either then, or now. Perhaps it would be better if you went,' said Cherrington rising from his chair.

'One moment, sir. If you are Mr Cherrington as you claim, then you will not have any objection if my constable makes a search of your rooms?'

'As a matter of fact I do. I consider that would be a gross infringement of personal property. This is all nonsense, Ravenscroft, utter nonsense. I have said quite plainly that you have confused me with this man Quinton. When you realize your mistake, I will be prepared to accept your apology.'

'Very neat, Captain Quinton,' smiled Ravenscroft.

'Will you stop calling me Captain Quinton. My name is Cherrington. I have always been Cherrington. I have never been this Quinton. I have poisoned no one. Now I suggest you go otherwise I will have recourse to my lawyer,' said Cherrington growing more and more angry.

'Ah, Mr Sefton Rawlinson, no doubt,' mocked Ravenscroft standing up and confronting his suspect.

'Who on earth is Sefton? For goodness sake, Ravenscroft, let's have an end to all this nonsense. I have an urgent appointment to keep at the bank.'

'Ah yes, your funds from India.'

'Yes, that is correct. Now if you will excuse me.'

'I don't believe there are any funds arriving from India. In fact, Mr Cherrington, I don't believe you have ever been to India let alone grown tea out there, or anywhere else for that matter,' said a heated Ravenscroft.

'You are quite wrong about all this, Ravenscroft, quite wrong.'

'I don't think so, Quinton. I suggest that my constable and I accompany you to your bank. We will see if these so called funds actually exist.'

'There is no need for all this.'

'Oh, I think there is. Would you like to lead the way Captain,' insisted Ravenscroft.

Cherrington gave a quick look of annoyance, and then a half smile, as he led the way out of the room.

* * *

'Ah good morning to you, Mr Cherrington,' said the clerk behind the counter.

'Good morning, Baylis. I understand that

181

my funds have arrived from Delhi?' asked Cherrington.

'Ah yes, sir. If you would care to wait a moment, sir, I will ask Mr Mortimer the manager to speak with you,' replied the clerk.

'That is most kind,' smiled Cherrington glancing in Ravenscroft and Crabb's direction. 'You will see that you have been mistaken in these slanders, Ravenscroft.'

The detective said nothing, but could not help feeling uneasy.

'Good morning Mr Cherrington,' said the manager appearing from the inner room and shaking his client's hand vigorously. 'And how may we be of assistance to you today?'

'I understand that my funds have finally been transferred from Delhi,' said Cherrington.

'I am sorry, I don't quite understand who these two gentlemen are?' asked the manager giving Ravenscroft and Crabb a suspicious glance.

'Forgive me, sir,' said Ravenscroft stepping forwards. 'My name is Inspector Ravenscroft and this is my colleague, Constable Crabb. We have been investigating the poisonings at Talbots' Lodging House.'

'Yes, we have heard about them. An awful business,' sympathized the manager.

'We have a number of people to interview

in our investigations, of whom Mr Cherrington is one,' continued Ravenscroft. 'Mr Cherrington claims that he has just returned from India, and that he is waiting for funds to be transferred from there. I wonder if you could be good enough to either confirm or deny this for us, Mr Mortimer?'

'I am sorry, but I cannot disclose private information concerning a client, inspector. That would be quite unethical, as I am sure you understand.'

'That is quite all right, Mortimer,' added Cherrington. 'I am quite happy for the inspector to be made fully aware of my financial activities. After all, I have nothing to hide.'

'Well yes sir, I am pleased to confirm that your funds from Delhi have finally arrived this morning. I can only apologize for the delay,' said the manager giving a slight bow.

'That is quite all right, Mortimer,' smiled Cherrington turning to face Ravenscroft.

'So it is true that Mr Cherrington is in receipt of funds from India?' asked a somewhat startled Ravenscroft.

'Of course, sir. I have just said so,' replied the manager.

'Thank you, Mortimer,' said Cherrington.

'If you would care to draw on them at any time my bank and staff are at your disposal.

We can also advise you on any investment you might care to make.'

'Thank you. I wonder if I could withdraw twenty pounds for today?' asked Cherrington.

'Of course, sir. Baylis, will you be so kind as to give Mr Cherrington twenty pounds,' instructed Mortimer.

'Yes, sir,' replied the clerk. 'How would you like the notes, sir?'

'Perhaps three five pound notes and the rest in ones, if you please.'

'Thank you, sir, and if there is anything else I can do for you now?' asked the manager.

'Well actually there is. I intend leaving Pershore at the end of the week. I will be travelling to London and staying for a while at my club. If you could transfer the remainder of my account to your branch in Piccadilly I would be obliged,' said Cherrington.

'Certainly, sir. If you would care to call in tomorrow I will have all the paperwork arranged,' smiled Mortimer giving another little bow.

'Thank you, Mortimer. Until then.'

The clerk rushed to open the door for Cherrington and the two detectives.

'Good day to you, sir,' said Ravenscroft addressing the manager as he began to leave the bank.

'Well, Ravenscroft, I hope that you are now

satisfied? Let us have an end to all this nonsense,' said Cherrington as the three men stood outside the building. 'Now if you will excuse me, I have a great deal to attend to before my departure. I wish you good day, sir.'

9

Pershore

'Confound the smug arrogance of the man,' grumbled Ravenscroft as he and Crabb downed a tankard of ale in one of the local hostelries.

'He certainly had an answer for everything,' said Crabb.

'The delight he took in humiliating us in that bank. I could have sworn that he had been spinning us a tale all about those funds coming from India, and now confound it, the whole things turns out to be true.'

'Forgive me for saying this, sir, but has the idea occurred to you that perhaps after all . . . well that you were . . . well,' began Crabb somewhat hesitantly.

'You mean am I mistaken, and is he really Cherrington? No. I am more than ever convinced that he was the same man I interviewed over twenty years ago in London concerning the *Pimlico Poisoning* case. What's more, if he was guilty then, he is almost certainly guilty now.'

'Right, sir.'

'I am sure he poisoned Jones because he had encountered the dead man at some time in the past, and that Jones threatened to expose him for the charlatan he is. Cherrington then had to poison Miss Martin as well because she had found out that he had killed Jones. I can see no other reason why any of the other residents of Talbots' would have committed the crimes,' replied a sullen Ravenscroft.

'Not even Mrs Jacobson?' suggested Crabb.

'Yes, I will acknowledge that there is something about that woman and her activities that concerns me, but there may be a perfectly reasonable and innocent explanation for her behaviour. No, I still believe that Cherrington, or rather Quinton, is our man. The problem is — how are we to confront him successfully with his crimes before we can extract a confession?'

'We could search his rooms, sir? If we discovered arsenic in his possession, we would have our man.'

'I think he would have Sefton Rawlinson, or his equivalent, onto us in no time, but the man is so devious he would in all probability have hidden the arsenic somewhere else. No, the only way we can hold him before he leaves the town would be to prove that he is Quinton and not Cherrington.'

'How do we do that, sir?'

'I don't honestly know, Tom. The whole thing is a complete mess. If only we could establish some link between Jones and Quinton in the past. Of course, we have been forgetting one thing in all of this — Jones wasn't the man's real name!' exclaimed Ravenscroft

'You mean the pocket watch?' asked Crabb.

'Exactly. The inscription in the pocket watch said, *Charles Murphy 1872*. Assuming that the watch was actually owned by Jones, then that poses the question — why did Murphy call himself Jones?'

'Because he was trying to conceal his real name?'

'Yes, and people usually change their names because they have something to hide. They think by assuming another identity they can escape the past. I wonder what the man was doing with that nasty looking Webley in his possession?'

'He could have been on the run from someone, and wanted the weapon to defend himself?'

'A possibility, Tom, or perhaps he was planning a daring robbery or something similar, a robbery in which the gun would have been needed? Then we have also forgotten that letter, the one that people thought he was always expecting. I wonder if it ever arrived?'

'If he had been on the run, why would he have been waiting for a letter. Would he not have wished to kept his whereabouts secret?'

'I don't know. Do you remember that fragment of a letter you found under the bed? I have it here still in my wallet,' said Ravenscroft taking out the item and spreading it on the table. '*S. WORCESTER. SEPTEMBER 12. 3.P.M.* What do you think that means, Tom?'

'Could have come from a letter sent to someone else? There's no knowing how long it had been under that bed?'

'Yes, I'm inclined to agree with you. It tells us nothing anyway. I don't know why I kept it,' sighed Ravenscroft.

'Is not the day after tomorrow September 12?'

'September 12?'

'The scrap mentions September 12.'

'I think you are right, Tom. It is the day after tomorrow. Was this part of a letter asking Jones/Murphy, to meet someone called 'S' in Worcester at three o'clock on that day? If that was the case, it does not say where in Worcester, nor why. I suppose that was on the remainder of the letter which has been destroyed.'

'What do we do now, sir?' asked Crabb.

'I want to know a lot more about this

Murphy — and there was also a name on that gun — 'John Elliott', or something like that. If we are seeking a link between this Murphy and our Quinton, then we need to dig deeper into the man's past. We will visit the telegraph office and send some urgent telegrams to my former colleagues at the Yard in London. Drink up, Tom.'

* * *

'Well that is done,' remarked Ravenscroft as he closed the door behind him and stepped out into the street.

'When can we expect a reply?' enquired Crabb.

'Hopefully by tomorrow. I told the authorities that the matter was of some urgency. If we are to detain Quinton we must have the evidence before he leaves the town for good. Once he moves to London it will be a great deal harder to track him down. In the meantime I think we will return to the bank and see if we can obtain any more information regarding Quinton from the manager but I think that might just have to wait,' said Ravenscroft as two familiar figures came slowly towards them.

'Good day to you, inspector,' said Miss Arabella Fanshaw.

'Good day to you, Miss Fanshaw, and Miss Fanshaw,' replied Ravenscroft raising his hat.

'Good day to you, inspector,' said Miss Clarisa Fanshaw. 'And a lovely one at that.'

'Indeed so, ladies.'

'And how are your investigations proceeding, inspector?' enquired Arabella.

'Well, thank you, ladies,' lied Ravenscroft. 'We have been able to recover some items belonging to the dead man, Jones.'

'How interesting,' said Arabella looking keenly at him.

'Yes, it seems that our Mr Jones was not called Jones at all. His pocket watch was engraved with the name 'Charles Murphy'. I don't suppose the name means anything to you ladies?' asked Ravenscroft.

'Charles Murphy, you say? No, I don't believe my sister, nor I, have any recollection of such a name,' said Arabella.

'Miss Fanshaw?' asked Ravenscroft turning towards the younger sister.

'No, inspector,' replied Clarisa.

'Thank you, ladies. We will of course inform you of any developments in the case,' added Ravenscroft.

'That is most kind of you. Thank you, inspector. We wish you a good day,' said Arabella.

Ravenscroft raised his hat once more as the

two sisters continued on their journey down the street.

'Delightful ladies,' said Crabb.

'Indeed. Come, let us continue to the bank. But wait a moment. Who is that there on the other side of the street?'

'Mrs Jacobson, if I'm not mistaken,' answered Crabb.

'She seems in quite a hurry,' said Ravenscroft as the figure receded into the distance. 'What time is it, Tom?'

'Just gone two, sir,'

'The time I believe that Mrs Jacobson is in the habit of taking her walk. Wait until she turns the corner, then we will follow her and see where she is going,' instructed Ravenscroft.

The two men walked quickly down the road and then peered cautiously round the corner building.

'There she is, sir,' indicated Crabb.

'She appears to be walking through the Market Place. We will need to keep a sharp eye on her, if we are not to lose her amongst the crowd of buyers,' said Ravenscroft.

'I think she is turning into one of the buildings,' said Crabb as the two men made their way through the busy market stalls.

'You're right and, if I am not mistaken, it is the Angel. She must be meeting someone there.'

192

'Shall we follow her inside?'

'Not at present. If she is meeting someone there, we need to know who it is. I think we should wait two or three minutes to allow time for this other person, who ever he or she is, to arrive. If we go in now and confront her, we may be too soon and it could warn the other person off.'

'She could be meeting Cherrington.'

'Or even our absent friend Claybourne, the insurance agent? Either way, we should know quite soon.'

After a few minutes had elapsed Ravenscroft and Crabb entered through the ornate doorway of the Angel Hotel.

'Good afternoon, sir. How can I be of assistance to you?' asked the young clerk standing behind the reception counter, who was busily engaged in writing in a large ledger. 'A room for the night, perhaps?'

'Good afternoon to you. In fact we would like some information regarding a young lady who entered your premises a few moments ago,' said Ravenscroft.

'To what young lady are you referring?' asked the young man adopting a more formal tone of voice, and displaying a slight twitch of the nose as he did so.

'A tall, dark-haired lady, by the name of Mrs Jacobson,' said Ravenscroft.

'I am sorry, sir, I have seen no one of that name enter our establishment,' replied the clerk looking down his nose at the two policemen.

'Come, my man, we have been watching your premises for several minutes now, and the only person to enter here during the past ten minutes has been Mrs Jacobson,' said Ravenscroft raising his voice.

'I'm sorry, sir, I cannot be of assistance to you,' said the clerk slamming the register closed. 'Our guests rely on our total discretion and confidentiality. Now if you will excuse me.'

'Just one minute, my dear sir. My name is Detective Inspector Ravenscroft and this is my assistant Constable Crabb,' said Ravenscroft.

'Well if you are policemen, as you say you are, why is your assistant not wearing a police uniform?' enquired the clerk casting a disparaging glance in Crabb's direction.

'Because when we are engaged in detective work it is not always necessary for my assistant to wear a police uniform; sometimes it is better if we are in plain clothes,' retorted Ravenscroft. 'Now sir, you have no doubt heard of the strange poisonings at Talbots' Lodging House? I thought so. Well that is what my colleague and I are investigating. We believe that one of our suspects entered this establishment not five minutes ago. Either you confirm our observation, and tell me where the young lady went, or I will search every room in this building until I find her. This would cause a great deal of disturbance to your other guests, but if it has to be done, then so be it. I trust I make myself plain in this matter?'

'Quite, sir. It was not my intention to withhold any information which might have been of police importance,' muttered the young man growing red in the face. 'But I can assure you that no one of the name of Jacobson has entered here. The lady who entered was a Miss Malltravers.'

'Malltravers. An interesting name. And how often does this Miss Malltravers visit your establishment?'

'About twice a week, sir, if I am not mistaken,'

'And where does this 'Miss Malltravers' go exactly?' asked Ravenscroft.

'I would rather not say, sir,' replied the clerk.

'Come now, sir, the truth if you please,' demanded Ravenscroft looking the clerk directly in the eyes.

'Well, sir. She usually goes to room number three. I'm afraid there is a gentleman involved.'

'There usually is,' remarked Ravenscroft. 'And what is the name of this gentleman if you please?'

'Mr Harris, sir.'

'Thank you, and where might we find this room?'

'First floor, go up the stairs, turn left, second door on the right,' replied the reluctant clerk. 'In fact the gentleman usually requests a bottle of whisky and some glasses to be sent up to his room. I was just about to take them up.'

'Thank you. Perhaps you would care to give them to me. I will see that they are safely delivered,' smiled Ravenscroft.

The clerk disappeared from view and returned a few seconds later carrying a small silver tray on which a bottle and two glasses were placed.

'Thank you,' said Ravenscroft taking hold of the tray.

'If I could emphasize discretion, gentlemen,' called out the clerk as Ravenscroft and Crabb quickly walked up the stairs. 'Discretion at all times if you would be so good.'

'Wonder who *Miss Malltravers* is meeting?' said Crabb.

'I don't know, but we shall soon find out,' replied Ravenscroft tapping lightly on the door.

'Yes?' called a voice presently from within.

'It is the waiter, sir. I have your refreshment, sir,' replied Ravenscroft adopting a different voice.

'Come.'

Ravenscroft pushed open the door and entered the room, closely followed by Crabb. A tall, thin, grey-haired man was seated on the bed, the buttons of his waistcoat undone. A woman faced the window, her back towards the room

'Put them on the table,' said the man.

The woman turned and let out a loud cry of surprise.

'Whatever is the matter?' asked the man jumping up off the bed.

'He . . . he is a policeman!' exclaimed a startled Mrs Jacobson.

'What the devil — ' began the man.

'My name is Detective Inspector Ravenscroft, and this is my colleague Constable Crabb,' said Ravenscroft.

'The devil you are! What do you mean by barging into a gentleman's bedroom like this?' demanded the man growing red in the face as he confronted Ravenscroft.

'We are investigating the deaths of two people in Pershore. This lady, Mrs Jacobson, is under surveillance as one of the suspects in the case. We followed her here today,' began Ravenscroft.

'Deaths? What deaths?' shouted the man.

'Two people have died in suspicious circumstances at Talbots' Lodging House, a gentleman by the name of Murphy, and a Miss Martin. I have questioned Mrs Jacobson about the poisonings, and as I have not been entirely satisfied with her answers, I considered it my duty to follow her here today.'

'Poisonings? What poisonings?' asked the man turning to face his distraught companion. 'You did not mention any of this to me.'

'I'm sorry, Hubert — ' began Mrs Jacobson.

'Silence woman!' reprimanded the man reaching out for his coat and walking briskly towards the door. 'If you will excuse me, gentlemen.'

'Crabb,' instructed Ravenscroft.

'Get out of my way, constable,' growled the man staring hard at Crabb who had positioned himself by the exit.

'Mr Harris, we need to ask you some questions before I can allow you to leave,' said Ravenscroft firmly.

'The deuce you will!'

'Sir, I have to remind you that two people are dead, Mrs Jacobson remains a strong suspect, and you may be complicit in these murders for all we know,' said Ravenscroft standing his ground as the man swung round and faced him in an aggressive manner.

'This gentleman has nothing to do with this matter,' intervened Mrs Jacobson.

'With all due respect, ma'am, that is for us to decide,' said Ravenscroft.

'Look here, Mrs Jacobson and I are great friends. We meet once in a while. I've never been to this Talbots' Lodging House, or whatever it is called, and I certainly know nothing of any murders. Now I would be obliged if your constable would let me go,' said Harris firmly.

'I would like to ask you some questions first, sir,' said Ravenscroft.

'Damn it, man! I would have you know that the Police Superintendent and I are good friends. I'll have a word with him later and settle this affair.'

'I would still like to ask you a few questions, sir,' continued Ravenscroft anxious to maintain his position.

Harris stared at Ravenscroft for a few seconds, and then reaching out towards the detective's arm said 'Look, Ravenscroft, I might have been a bit hasty. Would be obliged if we could have a quiet word together, just man to man as it were. Would not want to upset the lady, as I am sure you appreciate.'

'Very well, sir,' agreed Ravenscroft opening the bedroom door.

Ravenscroft and Harris stepped out into the corridor.

Harris closed the door behind him. 'Now see here, Ravenscroft, sorry for my abrupt behaviour in there. I can see you are a man of the world. Mrs Jacobson and I have been meeting here for the past year, usually once or twice a week. Neither of us would want this to get out. The lady is after all married and has a reputation to uphold, and I — well the least said about me the better. Let me just say that I have an important position to maintain in the county, and if this got out, tongues would wag. You know how it is. People are always putting two and two together, and drawing their own erroneous conclusions. If I give you my word that I know nothing about these deaths, I hope you would be gentlemanly enough to overlook this matter,' said Harris taking out his wallet from his coat pocket.

'Mr Harris, I trust that you will not open that wallet. It would be extremely uncomfortable for you if you did so,' said Ravenscroft.

'Your word against mine,' replied Harris replacing the wallet inside his pocket.

'All I require, sir, are some truthful answers to a few questions,' said Ravenscroft.

'Oh very well then, man,' sighed Harris. 'Let's get on with it. I have not got all day.'

'Thank you, sir. Overlooking the fact that 'Harris' is not your proper name, I would ask you how long you have known Mrs Jacobson?'

'For about six months, as I've just stated.'

'You are aware that the lady is still married?'

'Yes, yes, of course,' replied Harris showing signs of annoyance.

'Has Mrs Jacobson ever mentioned her husband to you?'

'She may have done, once or twice.'

'Were you and Mrs Jacobson planning to poison her husband, so that you could marry the lady?'

'Good heavens no!' laughed Harris. 'I am a respectable married man. As I said, I have an important position to maintain in society. I am not inclined to surrender all that to run off with some trollop.'

Ravenscroft smiled. 'You may like to know, sir, that we have caught Mrs Jacobson in possession of some arsenic powder.'

'Good grief!'

'She claims she uses it to improve her complexion.'

'Well yes, I suppose some women do. Look Ravenscroft, I give you my word that Mrs Jacobson has never mentioned anything concerning arsenic to me, and that certainly neither she nor I have any intention of poisoning either her husband, or anyone else for that matter. To tell you the truth, I am getting rather tired of all this secrecy. In fact I was going to end it all today. The rose has kind of lost its bloom, if you know what I mean,' said Harris winking his eye at Ravenscroft.

'Very well, sir.'

'Good man. I knew you would understand. I would be obliged if you would let me go now. I have rather an urgent meeting in Worcester to attend.'

'Mrs Jacobson?'

'I will let you make my excuses, if you will. Well Ravenscroft, happy to have been of assistance. Will see if I can put in a good word for you next time I see the Superintendent. Good day to you.'

Ravenscroft said nothing as he watched Harris walk quickly along the corridor and out of sight.

Returning to the room he found a distraught Mrs Jacobson seated on the bed, and Crabb staring out of the window.

'Has Lord . . . er Hubert left?' enquired the woman.

'Yes,' replied Ravenscroft.

'I see. I doubt I will ever see him again.'

'I would say, ma'am, that that is highly

likely. I have usually found that men in his position, once they have been found out in their indiscretion are only too anxious to avoid any scandal.'

'I suppose you will tell my husband?' asked Mrs Jacobson looking into the detective's eyes. 'I would be grateful if you did not.'

'I cannot promise that, Mrs Jacobson, but then I would be highly surprised if your husband was entirely unaware of your activities.'

'I only agreed to succumb to Hubert's attentions because I felt rather sorry for him. He is such a lonely, sensitive man.'

'Come now, Mrs Jacobson, you insult my intelligence. You and I both know the real reason why you and your so-called admirer meet twice a week in this bedroom,' said Ravenscroft.

'We have so few savings. My husband is unable to work. Lord . . . Hubert has been so kind to us.'

Ravenscroft smiled.

'Why have you followed me?' asked Mrs Jacobson rising from the bed.

'You are still a suspect in our investigations, Mrs Jacobson, and you have been caught in possession of arsenic. We knew that you had been meeting someone regularly, and it seemed a strong possibility that you and your 'admirer' might well have been plotting the death of your husband. Furthermore, it seems highly likely that the two of you may have poisoned both Mr Jones and Miss Martin because they learned of your assignation with this man.'

'All that is nonsense, inspector, as you well know. I would never do anything to harm my husband. I owe him my life. Yes, I have been one of your 'ladies of the night' when I lived in Whitechapel, and my life had almost come to an end when I met Ivan. My life had become so wretched. I had nothing, and one night I walked down to the river with the intention of ending it all. I was about to throw myself off the bridge when Ivan came up to me. He took care of me, taught me to value my own life and to escape from the mire into which I had sunk. I would do nothing to break that trust. I hope you understand that?'

'I think it would be better if you left, Mrs Jacobson,' said Ravenscroft unmoved by the woman's story.

Mrs Jacobson threw one more glance at Ravenscroft before quickly walking out of the room.

'Well, that's a surprise and no mistake,' said Crabb.

'People will sometimes resort to desperate

courses of action when faced with extreme difficulty.'

'I was half expecting your Captain Quinton to be here.'

'Yes. That would have been most convenient. Cherrington and Mrs Jacobson lovers, plotting to kill her husband, having previously been forced to kill Jones and Miss Martin because they had unearthed their little plot, but it was not to be.'

'Who's the gent?'

'Well his name is not Harris. Mrs Jacobson let out his first name, Hubert, that is all, and also that he is a Lord. Do you know, Tom, he had the affrontery to offer me money to hush all this up.'

'The nerve of the man. Do you believe all that sad tale of hers?' asked Crabb.

'There may be some truth in it, but that woman has lied to us so much, it is difficult to believe anything that she says now. Undoubtedly she only agreed to meet her so called lover here because he paid her for her attentions. I do not believe that they were planning to poison her husband. He would not have given up his wife and position for such a woman. That is why I decided to let the gentleman go. Well, now that we have satisfied our curiosity regarding Mrs Jacobson, I think we might return to our original intention of visiting the bank again to see if we can find out more concerning our main suspect.'

★ ★ ★

'Good day to you again. I would like a word with the manager if you please,' said Ravenscroft trying to sound as affable as he could.

The clerk gave him a disapproving stare, before disappearing into the inner room.

'Inspector Ravenscroft, I have told you all that I can about Mr Cherrington,' said Mortimer dismissively as he came out of his office.

'Nevertheless, sir, I would appreciate a few moments of your time. The matter is quite urgent, I can assure you.'

'Oh very well,' sighed Mortimer. 'You had best come into my office.'

Ravenscroft and Crabb followed the manager.

'If you would care to take a seat, inspector,' said Mortimer indicating a chair facing the desk.

'Thank you, sir.'

'Now how can I be of assistance to you?'

'As you are no doubt aware, Mr Mortimer, I am investigating the deaths of two persons

206

at Talbots' Lodging House. What I have to tell you now is in the strictest confidence, as I am sure you will appreciate. Our chief suspect in this case remains your client, Mr Cherrington. I believe, however, that this is not the gentleman's real name.'

'I see.'

'The gentleman's real name is Quinton. Many years ago he was the chief suspect in the *Pimlico Poisoning* case and, although acquitted on a technicality, the police firmly believed that a miscarriage of justice took place.'

'Yes, I see. Well yes, anything that I can help you with, inspector,' replied Mortimer looking anxious.

'Thank you, Mr Mortimer. What can you tell me about the gentleman's funds? Has the money really been transferred from India?'

'Oh yes, inspector, I can confirm that.'

'And the amount?'

'Three hundred and fifty pounds.'

'Not a vast fortune, but nevertheless a reasonably large sum. Have you have any further details regarding these funds?' asked Ravenscroft, keen to know more.

'One moment. Ah yes, I have the file here,' replied Mortimer looking through a pile of papers on his desk. 'Yes. Apparently most of the money came from the payment of a life assurance policy issued by the Bombay Life Assurance Company.'

'Really, that is most interesting. I don't suppose we have the name of the person who was covered by the policy?' asked Ravenscroft hopefully.

'I don't believe so, although, wait a moment. You may be in luck, inspector. Apparently the policy had been taken out on a certain Mrs Isabella Quinton.'

'Now that is most interesting,' smiled Ravenscroft.

'Seems as though you were right, sir,' said Crabb.

'Quinton and Cherrington are one and the same. Thank you, Mr Mortimer, you have been most helpful. There is one more thing that you could do for us.'

'Yes certainly.'

'Mr Cherrington has announced his intention of visiting you again tomorrow to sign the papers for the transfer of his funds to your branch in London.'

'That is so.'

'I would be grateful if you come up with some pretext or other to delay the signing of the papers. You see we intend questioning this gentleman after our conversation, and we would hope to elicit a confession from him. However it may take us some time to acquire the necessary proof to implicate him in these murders here in Pershore. If you could, therefore, delay the transfer of his funds, say until the day after tomorrow, that would ensure that Mr Quinton remains in the town until then. I would be unhappy if he left Pershore tomorrow before we have acquired the necessary evidence against him. I am sure that you understand our position, Mr Mortimer?' said Ravenscroft choosing his words carefully.

'Yes indeed. I can arrange that.'

'Then we are indebted to you,' said Ravenscroft standing up and warmly shaking the manager's hand.

*   *   *

'So, Tom, now we have him. Having poisoned his first wife all those years ago in Pimlico, and then most probably his second wife in India to acquire the insurance money, Quinton has now also poisoned two innocent residents of Talbots',' said Ravenscroft as he and Crabb hastened back towards the lodging house.

'You were right along, sir,' said Crabb.

'Quinton must have poisoned Jones, or Murphy as we now know he was called, because he had met the man somewhere in the past, and Jones had threatened to expose him.'

'And Miss Martin, sir?'

'She must have realized that Quinton had poisoned Jones, and then decided to blackmail him. That was why Quinton had to kill her as well.'

'Very neat,'

'Yes. I am sure that is the case. We will confront Cherrington with our news and see how he reacts. If we press him hard enough, we may be fortunate enough to get him to confess.'

'Let us hope so.'

'Perhaps we could tie up this case by the end of the day, and I would be free to join Mrs Ravenscroft in Weymouth. We live in hope, Tom. We live in hope.'

★ ★ ★

Ravenscroft tapped on the door.

'Oh for goodness sake, Ravenscroft, cannot you leave me alone? This is quite intolerable, man!' exclaimed Cherrington when he opened the door.

'We need to ask you some more questions, Mr Cherrington,' insisted Ravenscroft.

'I have told you all I can. You have seen how my funds have arrived from India, despite all your nonsense. I think I am quite in my rights to refuse to say any more about this matter,' said Cherrington attempting to close the door on the two arrivals.

'There has been a development in the case, Mr Cherrington, which directly affects you. I also have to remind you that we are still investigating two murders in this lodging house,' replied Ravenscroft firmly placing his hand on the opened door panel.

'What development?'

'May we come in, sir. It would be better if we could speak with you privately.'

'I will give you five minutes, Ravenscroft and that is all,' said Cherrington standing back from the door and allowing the two detectives to enter.

'I will come straight to the point, Mr Cherrington,' said Ravenscroft when he had seated himself. 'Do you still maintain that you are not Quinton?'

'This is ridiculous, Ravenscroft. I have already told you that my name is Cherrington and that I know nothing concerning this Quinton,' declared Cherrington sitting back in his arm chair and lighting a cigarette.

'So you keep saying, sir. Well I have to tell you that I have just visited your bank, and have had a most informative conversation there with Mr Mortimer. He was able to

211

confirm the transfer of your funds from India, but a close examination of the papers showed that the money had been claimed on an insurance policy issued by the Bombay Assurance Company — '

'You had the audacity to delve into my private papers!' interrupted Cherrington. 'You have gone too far this time, Ravenscroft.'

'The policy had been claimed on the life of a Mrs Isabella Quinton. Your wife I presume, Captain Quinton?' said Ravenscroft with affect.

'Damn you!' exclaimed Cherrington.

'So I think we can now cease all this pretence. How did your wife die, Captain?' asked Ravenscroft realizing that he now had the upper hand.

'All right, all right. I have a perfectly valid explanation for all this,' replied Cherrington moving uneasily in his chair.

'I would be quite happy to hear it,' said a satisfied Ravenscroft peering over the top of his glasses.

'Yes, I knew Quinton. He was my business partner in India. Shortly before he and his wife died of the wretched fever they took out insurance policies making me the beneficiary.'

'Oh, why sir would they have done that?'

'To secure the business, man, so that if one of us died then the other would be able to continue knowing that he was still financially solvent. I likewise took out an insurance policy on my own life, so that in the event of my demise, Quinton would have been able to carry on after me. It all made good business sense,' said Cherrington recovering his composure and puffing out smoke into the room.

'This is all nonsense, Quinton,' laughed Ravenscroft.

'It may seem nonsense to you, inspector, but if you had ever lived in India, and been surrounded by all the death and disease there, you would have seen the necessity for such insurance.'

'If all this is true, Mr Cherrington, why did you declare that you had never heard of anyone called Quinton when we questioned you?' continued Ravenscroft.

'I admit that does sound rather suspicious. One evening, in India, Captain Quinton told me the sad story of how he had been unjustly arraigned for the death of his first wife all those years ago in Pimlico, and how the police there had been mistaken in their investigations, and how he had been driven out of the country by false accusations after the trial. I, of course, sympathized with my poor friend's predicament. Naturally when the name of Quinton was raised by you in your questioning, I thought it prudent not to admit the association with Quinton. I could see how such an admission might easily lead you to suppose that I was that man, and with Quinton dead there was no way of proving otherwise,' said a confident Cherrington.

'This is all very neat,' said Ravenscroft taken aback by his suspect's new line of defence.

'I admit that it does not seem very plausible, inspector, but I can assure you that what I have just told you is the truth. I am not Quinton.'

'This is all nonsense, sir. Come now admit that you are Quinton,' insisted Ravenscroft.

'I do not know how to answer you, inspector, only to tell you that you are completely misguided in your persistence,' said Cherrington leaning back in his armchair before inhaling once again on his cigarette.

'I know you are Quinton and, furthermore, I know that you poisoned Jones,' said Ravenscroft beginning to feel unsettled by his suspect's assurance and calm.

'Oh come now, inspector. What possible motive could I have for killing poor Jones?'

'I believe that you and Jones — or rather Murphy, as we have now established this as his real name — had met somewhere previously, and that this gentleman had threatened to expose you as Quinton.'

'For goodness sake, man, that is quite ridiculous,' laughed Cherrington. 'And if I had been this Quinton, which I am not, why would I have wanted to kill Jones or Murphy? Quinton after all was innocent of his crimes, so he would have had nothing to fear from this man. There was nothing to be uncovered and certainly nothing of which to be ashamed. No, inspector, none of this holds up at all. I suppose you think I killed poor Miss Martin as well because I had met her sometime in the past?'

'And did you not poison the poor lady?' asked Ravenscroft becoming more frustrated by his lack of progress.

'Of course I didn't. Why would I have wanted her dead? Earlier today you said I was trying to marry the good lady for her money. Now you say I poisoned her because she had learnt of some terrible secret I possessed. Perhaps you should make up your mind, inspector. All of this is quite absurd. I really think that you need to take a holiday, Ravenscroft.'

'I know, Cherrington, that you are Quinton — and I know that you poisoned that young lady in Pimlico all those years ago, and that you have now poisoned Jones and Miss Martin,' said Ravenscroft with determination and mounting anger.

'Look, Ravenscroft there is a simple answer to all this. If you have enough evidence to prove all these wild accusations, then why don't you arrest me and put me on trial. Well?' taunted Cherrington. 'No, I thought not. I think you had better go, and arrest the real perpetrator of these crimes.'

'You may think you are very clever, Captain Quinton. I know that you cannot ever be tried again for the death of that poor innocent woman all those years ago, but I can assure you that I will find the evidence for your murders of Jones and Miss Martin, and that you will be brought to trial,' said Ravenscroft rising from his chair.

'Then I wish you well, inspector. I will be waiting for your return with eager anticipation,' smiled Cherrington.

Ravenscroft and Crabb quickly left the room, and closing the door behind them, walked silently down the stairs and out of the lodging house.

* * *

'The insufferable man!' said a frustrated Ravenscroft as he strode into the police station.

'Good afternoon, sir,' said Hoskings

216

standing to attention.

'There is nothing good about it, Hoskings,' growled Ravenscroft bringing his hand down hard on the counter.

'No, sir,' replied the startled constable.

'I thought we had him, sir. I was sure he was going to confess,' said Crabb trying to sound encouraging.

'All that nonsense about Quinton being his business partner! Lies all of it, damned lies! I know that he poisoned all three of them, and he knows that he has been acquitted on the first charge and that we have no evidence on the others. The conceit of the man,' muttered Ravenscroft striding up and down. 'What are we to do, Tom? How can I bring him to book?'

Crabb at a loss for words, looked down at his feet.

'Oh, this came for you, sir,' said Hoskings holding out an envelope.

'Reply from the Yard. They were quick regarding our inquiries,' replied a sullen Ravenscroft tearing open the envelope and reading the telegram. 'Nothing regarding our man Charles Murphy, but apparently Robertson is still alive and I have his address here.'

'Your old police inspector in Pimlico?' asked Crabb.

'The very same. I had thought him long

dead, but he is now living in Whitechapel of all places. I shall go and visit him tomorrow.'

'Whatever for, sir?'

'He will be interested to know that Quinton has emerged again after all these years, and, who knows, he may be able to tell me something further about the man that may help us in our investigations,' said Ravenscroft adopting a more energetic manner.

'What shall we do about Cherrington while you are away?' asked Crabb.

'You will remain here, Tom and keep a keen eye on the man. Hoskings here can assist you. Do not let him out of your sight.'

'What should I do if he attempts to leave the town?'

'Arrest the man and place him in the cells,' instructed Ravenscroft.

'On what charge, sir?'

'Oh anything, Tom. Anything you can think of. The main thing is, don't let him get away from us.'

'Right, sir.'

'Now, Hoskings, where is the Bradshaw?'

10

Whitechapel, London

Ravenscroft sat back in the railway carriage and watched the ever-changing countryside pass as the train made its way through the country towns of Worcestershire and onto the honey-stoned villages of Gloucestershire and Oxfordshire.

His thoughts turned to the previous evening when he had returned home late to Ledbury; he had entered the small cottage in Church Lane, the place which had been his home for the previous two years, and where he had come to value the happiness and warmth that his new life had brought him. The strangely quiet emptiness of the building had reminded him of the many years of futility and loneliness he had experienced in his previous existence in Whitechapel, and that painful recollection had weighed down heavily upon him, adding to the frustration and annoyance he had experienced earlier that day. He'd walked into the kitchen, where he had poured some water from the pitcher into a glass, before cutting himself two slices

219

of ham from the remainder of the previous day's joint, and he placed these between two pieces of bread. Taking this simple fare back into the living room, he had seated himself in his usual armchair and gazed into the empty fireplace. He half-expected that the quiet would be broken at any moment by the welcome return of his wife and children. When he finally climbed the stairs later that night it had been with a heavy heart that was full of unease and doubt, and when he had woken earlier the following morning, after an unsettled and restless night, he found his dark mood had not lifted. Now as the train left Oxford and drew closer to the metropolis it seemed almost as though his recent life was slowly ebbing away, and was being replaced by old familiar, gloomy memories that he had sought to forget.

Why had he chosen to seek out his old mentor Robertson after all these years? To bring the old man some satisfaction? To tell him that at last he had encountered Quinton and that their past failure to bring the man to justice might now be superseded by this new opportunity to make him pay for both his past and present crimes? Or was it simply that Ravenscroft was too aware that the man might be escaping justice yet again, and that only Robertson might now provide him with the reassurance and encouragement he needed to press on with his endeavours?

As the train slowed towards the end of its journey and passed the rows of dirty tenement buildings that spread monotonously along the sides of the track, Ravenscroft felt the sky had darkened with the smoke from a thousand chimneys, and he again wondered at the futility of his mission. Was he taking this opportunity to visit his old superior merely as a means of avoiding another confrontation with Quinton? Should he not have remained in Pershore instead and pursued his quarry there? Was this foolish adventure nothing more than an excuse not to face the inevitable? Failure had always been something which he could not face.

Stepping down from the train, he made his way along the congested platform, and through the bustling thoroughfare, out into the road where he hailed a passing cab.

'Where to, sir?' asked the dour cabman.

'Whitechapel, if you please,' replied Ravenscroft opening the door of the conveyance.

'What you want to go there? See the sights where all those murders took place?'

'No. I am seeking an old friend.'

'They never caught him you know.'

'Who?'

'Old Jack. That man ran rings rounds all

221

those idiot peelers.'

Ravenscroft allowed himself a brief smile as the cabman cracked his whip, and the vehicle sped away from the London terminus.

Alighting from the cab some minutes later, Ravenscroft handed the cabman some coins.

'Many thanks, governor. Mind how you go. Not a nice area this.'

'Thank you for your advice,' said Ravenscroft walking away from the cab and beginning to make his way along the once familiar streets. Although he had known the area for nearly twenty years, the noise, dirt and squalor of the place still came to him as a shock, as he realized that his near three year absence from there had softened his sensibilities.

Reaching a large red-brick house at the bottom of the street he knocked on the door.

'Yes. What do you want?' said an old woman with a red face and grubby hands who opened the door to him.

'I understand that Mr Robertson resides here,' said Ravenscroft.

'Straight up the steps, two flights, second door on left,' mumbled the woman wiping her hands on a dirty pinafore before turning on her heel and disappearing from view allowing Ravenscroft to enter the building.

He made his way up the two flights of

creaking steps, and reaching the landing he steadied his breathing before seeking out the door and tapping gently on the wood.

'Yes?' enquired a distant voice from within.

'Mr Robertson?'

'Yes, who is it?'

'An old friend. May I have a word with you?'

'Come in then,' replied the voice reluctantly.

Ravenscroft pushed open the door, stepped over the threshold, and found himself in a cramped, but simply furnished room. As he neared the light that shone forth from a warm, glowing fire situated at the far end of the room, he made out a huddled figure seated in an old armchair.

'Mr Robertson?' repeated Ravenscroft stepping nearer.

'Who the devil are you?'

Ravenscroft looked at the old grey-haired man seated in the chair, a grey rug wrapped round the lower half of his body and an old paisley shawl draped over his shoulders.

'It's Ravenscroft,' he replied.

'Ravenscroft?' coughed the old man.

'Yes, Ravenscroft. We served together in Pimlico, over twenty years ago. I was a constable then,' replied Ravenscroft hoping to awaken some recollection in his old superior.

'Ravenscroft? Come closer where I can see you. Ravenscroft you say? My God, it is Ravenscroft!' smiled Robertson before coughing loudly.

'I am glad to see you again, sir,' said Ravenscroft offering his hand which the old man shook limply.

'What are you doing now, Ravenscroft?'

'I left Whitechapel nearly three years ago. I am now a Detective Inspector at Ledbury in Herefordshire.'

'Well, you have done well,' said Robertson before indulging in a prolonged bout of coughing.

'Can I get you some water?' asked Ravenscroft.

Robertson pointed to a glass and jug on the table. Ravenscroft poured out some of the liquid into a glass, and handed it to the old man who brought it to his mouth with trembling hands.

'You find me unwell, Ravenscroft,' said Robertson leaning forwards and replacing the glass on the table. 'I am an old man now. Not like the old days. I seldom go out now. Moved here two years ago. Ledbury you say? Detective Inspector. I always knew you would do well. Take a seat. What brings you to Whitechapel, my boy? You're a long way from Ledbury.' The words came in short, breathless sentences.

'Do you recall the *Pimlico Poisoning* case?' asked Ravenscroft seating himself on an old wooden chair.

'*Pimlico Poisoning* case? How could I forget it,' coughed Robertson with bitterness in his voice. 'That case did for me. They wanted me out after that failure.'

'What did you do when you left the force?'

'Got as far away from London as I could. Went to Manchester. Joined a private detective agency and did some work for them for a few years, until the old complaint caught up with me and finished all that,' said Robertson before sneezing and blowing his nose.

'Would you like some more water?' asked Ravenscroft.

Robertson continued coughing as he pointed to a small cabinet in the corner of the room. Ravenscroft crossed the floor, opened the door and took out the bottle and two glasses that were inside and brought them back to the main table. He poured out some of the liquid into the two glasses, and handed one of them to Robertson, before resuming his seat at the old man's side.

'Ah, that's better,' said Robertson downing half the glass. 'Now where were we?'

'*The Pimlico Poisoning* case. You remember Quinton?'

'Quinton. How could I forget how that terrible man poisoned that young, innocent woman. We had him Ravenscroft, then he slipped through our fingers.'

'You never doubted his guilt?'

'Not for one minute. It was the diary that damned him. I can remember your reading it out when we questioned him. That last entry was all the evidence a jury would have needed to convict him, until that damned Rawlinson tore us to shreds. The man walked free. A grave injustice,' said a breathless, but angry Robertson before resuming his coughing.

'Well, I have some news of our Captain Quinton. At present I am investigating the deaths of two people in the town of Pershore. Both were poisoned. When I interviewed the people residing in the same lodging house as the deceased, I found that one of them was Quinton,' said Ravenscroft.

'The devil is back!' exclaimed Robertson.

'Calls himself Cherrington now. Told us some long tale about being out in India for five years, growing tea of all things. The interesting thing though is that he seems to have inherited a sum of money on his wife's life assurance policy.'

'Probably married her and poisoned the poor woman for the money, just like the first one.'

'My thoughts exactly.'

'And now you say he has poisoned two other people.'

'Yes.'

'Then why have you not arrested him, my boy?' asked Robertson before coughing loudly again and covering his mouth with his handkerchief.

'Because he denies he is Quinton, and because no one saw him do it,' replied Ravenscroft topping up Robertson's glass with the brandy from the bottle.

'And I suppose you have questioned him and tried to break him?'

'Yes, but to no avail. Just when we feel that we are getting close to extracting a confession from the man he turns the tables on us and comes out of it as fresh as a daisy,' sighed Ravenscroft.

'I see your predicament, Ravenscroft. What can I do to help?'

'I don't really . . . well I suppose what I really want is your backing or support,' mumbled Ravenscroft.

'You are beginning to have doubts?'

'No, not at all. I know that this man is Quinton, and I am sure that he is responsible for these poisonings.'

'Then you must go all out to get the man. Question him again. Break him down. Don't let him get away with it this time, Ravens-croft,' said Robertson gripping Ravenscroft's arm and staring intently at him through his watery, reddened eyes. 'I have waited over twenty years to bring that man to justice.'

'I know, but if there is no evidence against him?'

'Then you must find it, and if you cannot secure it, then you must make it,' urged Robertson coughing again before taking another drink of the brandy.

Ravenscroft turned away deep in thought.

'Look, Ravenscroft, you and I both know that he poisoned his first wife most cruelly, and that he has probably done away with others over the years, and now he has poisoned two others in Pershore or whatever it was. You cannot let him get away with it again. Tell me you will put him away this time, Ravenscroft. Promise me,' implored Robertson becoming increasingly agitated.

'I will,' replied Ravenscroft.

'Good man. Then I can finally die a satisfied man,' sighed Robertson sinking back into the chair.

'I am sure you will not die for many years yet,' said Ravenscroft trying to sound reassuring.

'Don't patronize me, Ravenscroft. I have seen the doctors. I only have a week or so left if I am fortunate,' coughed Robertson.

'I am sorry for it. I see that I have tired you. I apologize. I should take my leave,' mumbled Ravenscroft feeling uneasy, and not knowing what to say, as he stood up.

'It was good to see you, my boy. Good of you to come,' said Robertson in a voice that seemed to Ravenscroft to be scarcely more than a whisper.

'The honour was all mine.'

'See that you send him down, Ravenscroft. I will be counting on you.'

'I will.'

The old man closed his eyes as his head sank onto his chest.

Ravenscroft waited for a minute and then, realizing that he could do no more, slipped quietly from the room.

11

Pershore

It was with a new resolution that Ravenscroft set out for Pershore the following morning, having slept soundly the night after his return from the capital.

'And how was your old colleague?' asked Crabb as the horse and trap crossed over the bridge at Upton on their way to Pershore.

'Not well I am afraid. It seems that the illness which has long plagued him will shortly claim its victim,' replied Ravenscroft.

'I am very sorry, sir.'

'Nevertheless I think it was of some comfort to him to know that we have Quinton within our grasp once again. I am convinced more than ever now that Cherrington, or rather Quinton, is responsible for the deaths of Miss Martin and Jones.'

'How can we prove it, sir?' asked Crabb somewhat tentatively.

'I intend searching his rooms from top to bottom until I find the evidence. Then we will arrest him and take him to the police station. Perhaps a certain amount of prolonged hard questioning in a small, cold room will elicit a confession from him. I will not give up until I have that man hanging from a noose. I owe it to Robertson before he dies,' said a determined Ravenscroft.

After a few more miles of travel the cab drew up outside the lodging house.

'Hm, Talbot's sign appears to be in a sorrier state; about to fall on someone at any moment,' said Ravenscroft as he strode up to the front door and rang the bell.

'Good morning to you, sir,' said Maisie.

'Good morning, Maisie. Is Mr Cherrington at home?'

'Yes sir.'

'Good. We will see ourselves up. I think it would be advisable if Mr Talbot were to mend his sign outside the premises before it kills someone and we have another murder on our hands. Has Mr Claybourne returned yet?' asked Ravenscroft stepping into the hall.

'No, sir.'

Ravenscroft and Crabb marched up the two flights of stairs and banged on Cherrington's door.

'Ah Mr Ravenscroft, come to arrest me have you?' said Cherrington with sarcasm after he had opened the door and observed the two policemen.

'I have come to make a search of these

rooms, Mr Quinton,' said Ravenscroft pushing past the man.

'I object most strongly. This is insufferable,' protested Cherrington.

'You may protest as much as you like sir, but I have reason to believe that you are concealing vital evidence. You would oblige me sir by accompanying my constable here to the police station, whilst I undertake this search.'

'The devil I will!'

'Crabb, put the bracelets on him,' instructed Ravenscroft.

'Look here, Ravenscroft, there is no need for that.'

'Mr Quinton, either you now accompany Constable Crabb to the police station, under your own free will, and wait for me there until I have conducted this search or, if you continue to hinder our investigations, my constable will take you there in handcuffs. I do not think you would wish to be seen being led off to the police station handcuffed like a common felon,' said Ravenscroft firmly facing his suspect.

'Oh, very well Ravenscroft. I will go with your constable to the station. I choose not to go under duress because it amuses me to see how much more of a foolish ass you can make of yourself with this absurd behaviour,' taunted Cherrington.

'Crabb,' said Ravenscroft.

'You won't find anything here. A complete waste of time, Ravenscroft,' called out Cherrington as he and Crabb made their way onto the landing.

Ravenscroft closed the door and began his search.

The wardrobe and chest-of-drawers in the small bedroom revealed a number of suits and clothes, mainly of an expensive nature. Ravenscroft searched all the pockets for any pieces of paper that would yield information about his suspect, and emptied all the drawers to see if any items had been hidden there, but he found nothing. Next he turned his attention to the bed where after stripping back the sheets, he looked intently underneath the mattress and beneath the brass bedstead itself.

He then returned to the living room and turned his attention towards the collection of books on the sidetable, but was disappointed that there was no diary nor were there any other papers of a personal nature. The few volumes of Dickens and Trollope likewise failed to contain any annotations or dedications, and when he flicked through the pages he was disappointed to find no cuttings or loose pieces of paper enclosed within.

Sighing, Ravenscroft stared round the living room to see if there was anything else of interest. The landscape painting of some cows and sheep by a stream, he concluded had hung in its present position for a great many years, and the contents of a small silver tray that lay on the table consisted merely of some cigarettes and a folded copy of that day's edition of The Times.

Turning his attention towards the fireplace, he observed that, although the logs were cold, there was a charred collection of burnt papers in the hearth where their owner had set fire to them the previous day. Clearly Cherrington had destroyed anything of a personal nature that might have incriminated him. Ravenscroft realized that he had come too late, and cursed himself for not having carried out the search earlier. Now there would only be the questioning of his suspect that could solve the mystery.

Ravenscroft walked towards the door, but stopped when he noticed that Cherrington's silver-topped walking stick lay in the stand by the door. He picked up the item and, observing that there was a faded monogram engraved on the handle, he took the stick over to the window so that he could examine the letters more clearly.

'C.Q.!' exclaimed Ravenscroft out loud.

'Charles Quinton. I wonder what you will say now, Mr Cherrington?'

Grasping the stick, Ravenscroft made his way out of the room and down the stairs, and eagerly along the streets of the town towards the police station.

'Good morning, Hoskings. Where is the prisoner?' asked Ravenscroft addressing the constable who was standing behind the counter.

'With Constable Crabb in the backroom, sir,' answered the policeman.

Ravenscroft opened the door to reveal Cherrington seated at the table and Crabb standing by the door.

'I hope you are satisfied, Ravenscroft, now that you have searched my rooms. I presume you found nothing?' said Cherrington with his usual air of confidence.

'I see, Quinton, that you had been busy yesterday burning papers in your hearth,' replied Ravenscroft.

'It is not a crime to get rid of unwanted items.'

'Unless of course they are of an incriminating nature.'

'How are we to know, inspector?' smiled Quinton rising from his chair. 'In view of the fact that you have been unable to discover any arsenic, pistols, knives, or anything else of

235

a criminal nature in my rooms, I believe I am in my rights to wish you both a good day.'

'If you are leaving us, Mr Quinton, I am sure that you will require this,' said Ravenscroft laying the walking stick down on the table.

Cherrington said nothing as he stared down at the stick.

'Do please pick up the stick, Mr Quinton. You will observe that it has an inscribed monogram on the handle. 'C.Q.' Now I wonder what those letters represent? Perhaps you would care to enlighten us, Captain Quinton?' said Ravenscroft.

'You know perfectly well what they represent,' said Cherrington.

'Yes, 'Charles Quinton'. Shall we stop this pretence, captain? Sit down,' instructed Ravenscroft.

For a brief moment Ravenscroft thought he detected a look of anger crossing over his suspect's face.

'Look, old boy, there is a perfect explanation for all this,' said Cherrington resuming his usual air of light-heartedness as he resumed his seat.

'I should certainly like to hear it, Mr Quinton,' said Ravenscroft wondering how his suspect would explain away this item of evidence.

'It is all quite simple. When Quinton died

in India, I naturally thought that I would take over his walking stick. It was too good to discard, and Quinton had no relatives or other beneficiaries to leave it to. It would have been foolish to have discarded it.'

'Oh come, Captain Quinton, you surely do not expect us to believe that?' said Ravenscroft leaning back in his chair and observing his suspect intently.

'It is the truth. It is entirely up to you, inspector whether you believe me or not,' said Cherrington with an air of disdain.

Ravenscroft said nothing as he looked across at Crabb.

'Well if that is all?'

'Empty out your pockets, captain.'

'Whatever for?'

'I wish to make a search of your pockets. If you do not oblige us, sir, I will instruct my constable to carry out the search on my behalf,' said Ravenscroft with determination.

'No need for that, old boy,' replied Cherrington placing his hand in a coat pocket and bringing forth a number of items which he placed on the table. Ravenscroft searched through the numerous coins, and lifted up the silver cigarette case, which he examined carefully for any inscriptions.

'This case has been inscribed with the name *Charles Quinton!*' said Ravenscroft holding up the item.

'Very well. I confess it. I also took Quinton's cigarette case. It would only have been thrown away, or one of the servants would have taken it. Looks as though you will have to charge me with theft, inspector,' said Cherrington.

Ravenscroft sighed, knowing that his adversary was enjoying their confrontation.

'Sorry to have disappointed you, Ravenscroft.'

'Your wallet, sir.'

'Come now, Ravenscroft, surely some things can remain private?'

'Your wallet if you please, Captain Quinton,' said Ravenscroft firmly, but knowing that this was probably his last opportunity to obtain an admission from his chief suspect.

Cherrington reached into the top inside pocket of his coat and took out his wallet. 'There are just a few notes, a receipt from Talbot for the room, nothing more,' he said handing over the items to Ravenscroft.

'I should like to see the rest of the wallet if you please.'

Cherrington looked away quickly, as Ravenscroft reached for the wallet and peered inside.

'I told you there was nothing else there,' said Cherrington.

Ravenscroft ran his hand inside the empty wallet. 'Ah, what have we here, Mr Cherrington? There appears to be something behind the lining.'

Cherrington moved uneasily in his chair as Ravenscroft took out a small piece of folded paper which he then proceeded to open.

'A rather faded newspaper account headed *Pimlico Poisoner: Acquitted*'. Well, Captain Quinton this is most interesting. I suppose you are going to tell me that this was Captain Quinton's wallet, and that you appropriated it for yourself, and that you did not know that this newspaper cutting was here, hidden in the lining? However, you and I know that will not suffice, especially as the wallet has the name *Cherrington* neatly engraved on the outside,' said a triumphant Ravenscroft. 'It is all over with you, Captain Quinton!'

'All right, all right. Stop going on, man,' protested Ravenscroft's suspect burying his face in his hands. 'Yes, I am Captain Charles Quinton.'

'Thank you, sir. You should have discarded the cutting, like all the other papers you destroyed,' said a satisfied Ravenscroft.

'What do you want from me, Ravenscroft?' asked a crestfallen Quinton.

'The truth, Captain Quinton. That is all we have ever wanted.'

Quinton reached for the glass of water on the table and after swallowing its contents he turned to face his accusers. 'I remembered you Ravenscroft, that first day we met on the stairs at Talbots', as that young policeman who had arrested and charged me with the death of my first wife all those years ago in Pimlico, but I hoped that you would not recognize me. After the trial I attempted to resume my position in London society, but everywhere I went people were whispering behind my back or shunned me until I was driven out of the capital. For a while I tried living in Manchester and Liverpool, and then retired to the country, but it was the same everywhere I went. Then I decided to go to India. I thought that perhaps no one out there would have ever heard of the *Pimlico Poisoning* case. I started the tea plantation and the business prospered. I met and married Isabella, and we were happy for some years, until the fever took her away from me. Realizing that there was nothing left for me in India, I decided to return to England, but thought it better if I took the name Cherrington — it is an old name from my mother's side of the family — so that I could begin again, without the past haunting me. That is why I tried to make you believe that I was Cherrington, but you persisted with your

240

questions, never accepting what I was telling you, always trying to dig up the past. Why couldn't you leave things alone, Ravenscroft?'

'The answer to that, Captain Quinton, is that two murders have been committed here in Pershore. When and where had you previously encountered Jones, or should I say Murphy?'

'Good God, man, why will you not believe me when I tell you that I had nothing to do with that man's death? I had never seen him anywhere before. You must believe that,' pleaded Quinton.

'I believe that you poisoned Jones because he was threatening to expose you as Quinton — '

'No, no,' protested Quinton.

'And that you then poisoned Miss Martin because she was blackmailing you,' persisted Ravenscroft.

'No, no. This is all nonsense,' replied Quinton covering his face with his hands once more.

'Is it?'

'Look, Ravenscroft, I have never hurt anyone in my life. I did not poison my wife in Pimlico. I was aquitted by the jury and walked away from the Old Bailey as a free man. I came here to Pershore upon my return to England, because the place held fond memories for me and because I was waiting for my funds to arrive from India. I had never seen either Jones or Miss Martin before, and I certainly had nothing to do with their deaths.'

'Well, I have to tell you, Captain Quinton, that I do not believe you.'

'I know it was stupid of me to deny that I was Quinton. I realize that now. But if I had told you the truth you would naturally have concluded that I had committed these murders.'

'Why don't you tell me everything, Quinton?' said Ravenscroft leaning forward in his seat and looking directly at his suspect. 'You and I both know the truth. Surely you must be tired of all these lies and deceit. Why don't you confess that you killed Jones and Miss Martin?'

'Good heavens, man, why don't you believe me when I tell you I am innocent?' pleaded Quinton.

'You have lied to us so many times, Mr Quinton. Why should I believe you now?'

Quinton said nothing as he stared at the blank wall to his side for several moments. Ravenscroft was content to wait, knowing that it would only be a matter of time before he would, at last, secure a confession.

Suddenly Quinton rose to his feet. 'I have

to tell you, Ravenscroft, that I am innocent of these crimes. It is a pity that you cannot accept my word on this matter. As you have no further evidence against me, I believe that I am within my rights to walk away from this room. If you seek to detain me on these false accusations I will contact my lawyer, Mr Sefton Rawlinson, who will no doubt secure my release.'

'I do not like being threatened, Mr Quinton,' said Ravenscroft taken aback by this renewed assertiveness of his prime suspect.

'If you can find the evidence against me, then by all means charge me. Otherwise it is my intention to leave this town tomorrow. I wish you good day, Ravenscroft,' said Quinton picking up his cane and wallet and walking quickly towards the door.

'Sir?' said Crabb taken aback by this sudden turn in events.

'Let him go, Constable Crabb.'

Crabb stood aside as Quinton strode out of the room and on through the outer room of the police station.

'Shall I go after him, sir,' asked a perplexed Crabb.

'No use, Tom,' sighed Ravenscroft.

'But you and I both know he is guilty,' protested Crabb.

'Yes, and he knows that as well, but with no evidence to bring against the man . . . I was sure that once we had made him confess that he was Quinton all along, he would have admitted the poisonings as well.'

'He should have thrown that cutting away.'

'His vanity made him keep it. Damn it, Tom, every time I get close to extracting a confession from the man, he slips through our fingers yet again. I am afraid time is against us. Unless I can find the evidence that Quinton killed Jones and Miss Martin we shall lose him for good after tomorrow. There has to be some previous connection between Quinton and Jones. There just has to be — but where Tom, where?'

Crabb looked away, desperate that he could bring no comfort to his friend and superior.

'Right, Tom. Enough of this gloom. Let us repair to the local inn and refresh ourselves. Perhaps the ale there might give us new inspiration.'

★ ★ ★

'Here you are, sir. Two tankards of our finest ale. I will bring over the bread and ham to your table.'

'Thank you, landlord. We are certainly in need of these,' said Ravenscroft raising the tankard to his mouth. 'That is better. You seem very quiet in here today.'

'Gone to Worcester most of them,' replied the landlord wiping down the bar.

'Oh, why is that?' asked Ravenscroft.

'Haven't you heard. Lord Salisbury is speaking there.'

'I see.'

'Big rally by all accounts. You knows who Lord Salisbury is?'

'Of course.'

'Not everyday that the Prime Minister of England visits the county.'

'No, I suppose not.'

'It's all here in the paper,' said the landlord passing over the newspaper to Ravenscroft.

'*Lord Salisbury, Prime Minister to Address Anti-Home Rule Rally at Guildhall in Worcester at three o'clock this afternoon,*' read out Ravenscroft.

'Should be a grand occasion,' added the landlord.

'Indeed. Good God, Tom!' exclaimed Ravenscroft suddenly. 'We have been so stupid! That was on that slip of paper we found under Jones's bed: '*S.WORCESTER. SEPTEMBER 12. 3 P.M.*' Don't you see — 'S' stands for Salisbury, and the rest refers to the time and place of this rally — Worcester at three o'clock this afternoon.

What time is it now?'

'Just gone two, sir,' replied a startled Crabb.

'Quickly, get the trap!'

'Where are we going to, sir?'

'To Worcester with all possible speed. I pray we may yet be in time!'

12

Worcester

'I still don't understand, sir,' said Crabb as the trap set off at a fast pace along the road to Worcester.

'I should have seen it earlier. The pistol, the letter, the name Murphy, it all points to the Fenians,' replied Ravenscroft.

'You mean those Irish nationalists?'

'Yes. Some years ago they tried to blow up Clerkenwell gaol in London killing twelve people I believe in the process. They also tried to blow up the Yard though no one was killed that time. They will stop at nothing to secure Home Rule for Ireland.'

'Where does Lord Salisbury fit into all this?' asked Crabb.

'Well, a few years ago, the Liberals led by old Gladstone tried to get Home Rule through the House of Commons, but they were defeated by the Conservatives. Lord Salisbury, the present Conservative Prime Minister, is apparently visiting Worcester today to speak at an Anti-Home-Rule rally. I think Murphy was a Fenian, or certainly someone sympathetic to the Irish cause. I am sure that letter was instructing him to attend the rally and attempt an assassination of Lord Salisbury. You have seen the pistol, Tom.'

'But why are we trying to get to Worcester in time for the rally? Surely there is no urgency now that Jones, or rather Murphy, is dead.'

'Yes that is true, but we cannot conclude that the threat has been removed simply because Murphy is now dead. It could be that Murphy had an accomplice, or that the brotherhood are aware that Murphy is dead, and are sending someone else to carry out the attack. We cannot sit idly by when the life of the Prime Minister of this country may still be in danger,' explained Ravenscroft with determination.

'I see. Then I had better make this old horse go faster. There is another cab behind us that seems intent on keeping up close to us.'

'Don't worry about him. If there is an accomplice, and we can apprehend him before he has the opportunity to carry out his foul deed, we may also be able to discover the connection between Murphy and our Captain Quinton. Faster, Tom, faster.'

★ ★ ★

Crabb tied the reigns of the horse to a post outside the Commandery, and he and Ravenscroft set off at a brisk pace up the hill towards the cathedral.

'Ten minutes before Lord Salisbury is due to speak and it looks as though the world and his wife have decided to come to Worcester today,' said Ravenscroft observing the crowds of people who were intent on making their way along the narrow streets. 'When we arrive I will find the superintendent and alert him to the situation.'

The two policemen entered the main street of the town and pushed their way through the crowd towards the Guildhall.

'There he is,' said Ravenscroft pointing towards a uniformed officer who was walking up and down the pavement.

'Good morning, Ravenscroft. I thought you were still in Pershore investigating those poisonings,' said the Superintendent.

'I was, but important information has just come to hand to suggest that one of the deceased was a member of the Fenian Brotherhood,' said Ravenscroft anxious to impart his information as quickly as possible.

'Good grief!'

'We think he may have had an accomplice. I think we should stop the meeting.'

'Can't do that now, Ravenscroft. There will

be a riot if the meeting is called off at this short notice. I doubt we could stop it in time, anyway. All I can do is go round the men and alert them to the danger, and tell them to arrest any suspicious characters. Keep me informed, Ravenscroft,' said the superintendent, moving swiftly away.

'Who are we looking for, sir?' asked Crabb.

'I don't know, Tom. This Fenian could be anyone. All we can do is keep a sharp lookout for anyone behaving strangely,' replied Ravenscroft looking all around him. 'Listen to that, Tom. Do you hear the sound of a violin? I recognize that tune.'

'Turco,' pronounced Crabb.

'Quickly over there, by the wall,' pointed Ravenscroft.

The two policemen pushed their way through the crowd to where a familiar figure could be seen playing his violin, a hat containing coins at his feet.

'So, Count, we meet again,' said Ravenscroft. 'Empty your pockets if you please.'

'What is this? Who disturbs the Paganini?' shouted a startled Turco.

'Crabb, search the man,' instructed Ravenscroft.

'What you do? Turco he has done no harm,' protested the violinist.

'Nothing, sir,' said Crabb after searching

through the man's pockets.

'Nevertheless I want this man taken into custody,' said Ravenscroft calling over one of the constables who was standing nearby.

'This is not-a right,' said Turco.

'Constable, will you be so good as to arrest this man and take him under close supervision to the station,' said Ravenscroft.

'Yes sir. Now you just come along with me, sir,' replied the constable taking hold of Turco's arm and beginning to lead him away.

'What is this? You cannot do this to Turco,' shouted the musician as he disappeared into the crowd with the uniformed officer.

'You think Turco is part of this plot?' asked Crabb.

'I don't know. There was no weapon on him. Let's see if we can get nearer the front.'

The crowd suddenly surged forwards and cheered loudly as a group of dignitaries emerged from the main entrance to the Guildhall building and mounted the wooden stage that had been erected there.

A tall, grey-haired gentleman stepped forwards and introduced one of the speakers. 'Lord Parkinson, the chairman of the County Conservative Association, will now say a few words.'

'It's him!' exclaimed Crabb. 'He was the man in the hotel bedroom.'

'So I see. Said his name was Harris. No wonder he was anxious not to tell us who he really was. Afraid of the scandal. That must be Salisbury in the middle of the group,' said Ravenscroft attempting to push his way towards the front of the crowd.

Parkinson began speaking as the two detectives edged their way closer to the stage, both men looking intently at the people around them.

'Police, make way!' said Ravenscroft clearing a pathway until he and Crabb reached the front of the meeting. Then he and Crabb faced the crowd as the speech continued.

'One of these has to be the assassin,' whispered Ravenscroft.

'But which one?' asked Crabb as he surveyed the large crowd.

'Will you now welcome the Prime Minister, Lord Salisbury,' announced Parkinson as the crowd cheered enthusiastically.

Suddenly someone in the audience shrieked. Ravenscroft caught sight of what seemed like a glint of sunlight reflected off a bright object from somewhere in the midst of the crowd.

'Arrest that man!' shouted Ravenscroft pushing his way frantically towards the disturbance.

The crowd let out a number of cries as Ravenscroft saw the man taking aim.

'Stop that man!' cried Ravenscroft almost

within striking distance of the assassin.

'I have him!' yelled a voice in the crowd.

'No you aint,' shouted another.

'Over there!' cried a third voice.

Ravenscroft pushed forwards and attempted to wrench the weapon from the man's hand.

More members of the crowd cried out as Ravenscroft wrestled the man to the ground, but as he sought to secure him, the man forcibly pushed him to one side and quickly disappeared from view.

'Where is he?' shouted Ravenscroft getting quickly to his feet.

'Over there!' called out Crabb.

Ravenscroft and Crabb pushed their way frantically through the crowd as Parkinson was heard calling for order from the stage.

'Where has he gone?' said Ravenscroft emerging from the other side of the crowd.

'There, sir!' indicated Crabb pointing to a figure who was running along the road in the direction of the cathedral.

Ravenscroft and Crabb set off in quick pursuit and soon left the throng of people behind them as they chased the gunman across the green in front of the cathedral and round the side to the close.

'He must be making for the river,' said a breathless Ravenscroft observing that the man was now running down the flight of steps at the end of the cathedral close.

The two detectives followed the man down to the side of the river bank.

'There he is, sir. He must be making for the boats at Diglis,' shouted Crabb.

Ravenscroft could feel his chest tightening and his breath coming in short gasps as he and Crabb slowly gained on the man.

Suddenly the man stopped and turned to face the two detectives.

'Stop! If you come any nearer I will fire,' said the man pointing his gun at Ravenscroft.

'It is all over,' said Ravenscroft. 'You cannot escape.'

'I warn you, back away or I will fire.'

'Don't be a fool man. Give yourself up,' urged Ravenscroft as he inched closer, feeling a cold sweat running down his back as he looked the gunman in the eye.

'I tell you, I will fire!,' shouted the man levelling the gun at Ravenscroft.

Suddenly a shot rang out.

The man dropped the gun and fell to the ground, crying out in pain as he did so, and clutching his wounded arm.

Ravenscroft spun round to see where the shot had come from, and saw a tall, dark-haired man holding a smoking revolver in his hand, and two uniformed policemen running up behind him.

'What!' exclaimed a relieved but perplexed Ravenscroft.

'Take hold of him, men,' instructed the man addressing the constables. 'Are you all right, Ravenscroft?'

'Yes,' replied the startled detective. 'Who the devil are you, and how do you know my name?'

'Permit me to introduce myself. My name is Forbes from the Yard. Section D, Special Branch.'

The policemen pulled the wounded gunman to his feet.

'Take him to the station,' continued the new arrival.

'Special Branch? I don't understand?' said a bewildered Ravenscroft as the blood-stained man was led away.

'I am part of a special unit that has been established at the Yard to counter the Fenians. Charles Murphy has been one of our chief suspects for quite a while now. Recently we discovered that he had travelled to America to obtain guns and money there. When your telegram arrived at the Yard requesting information regarding Murphy, we knew that he must have arrived back in the country, and that he had evidently been planning some atrocity before his demise. Although your message stated that Murphy was dead, we knew that he had accomplices. We were also aware that Lord Salisbury was speaking here today,' explained Forbes quickly.

'Well I'll be blowed!' exclaimed Crabb.

'I decided to travel down to Pershore early this morning and observed you taking a man to the police station for questioning. I then followed you to the inn and overheard your conversation there.'

'I did not notice you.'

'That was my intention. We pride ourselves at Special Branch in following our suspects without causing suspicion,' smiled Forbes. 'When you set off for Worcester, I followed you as quickly as I could.'

'So it was you in that cab behind us?' said Ravenscroft.

'The gunman goes by the name of Flannigan. He is on our list of Fenian sympathizers.'

'Well I am certainly glad that you arrived when you did. I do not know if I would have reached that gun before he fired it.'

'I doubt it. That is why I shot him. The man is only wounded in the arm. We will attend to his wound. Then I will take him back to London for further questioning. He will no doubt recover in time to be hung. You have done good work, Ravenscroft. I will see that the authorities hear about it. I wish you good day, sir,' said Forbes turning away.

'One moment, sir. I am still investigating two murders in Pershore. One of the victims was your suspect Murphy, or Jones as he called himself. My chief suspect is a man by the name of Charles Quinton, although he also goes by the name of Cherrington. I have reason to believe that Murphy and my suspect met somewhere in the past, and that Quinton killed Murphy because of that association,' said Ravenscroft.

'The names of Quinton and Cherrington mean nothing to me,' said Forbes dismissively.

'Nevertheless, Mr Forbes I would like to question your suspect Flannigan. He might be able to provide us with vital information regarding my case,' said Ravenscroft.

'I am not sure that will be possible. Flannigan is a dangerous character and we need to question him as soon as possible. He may have important information to tell us regarding the safety of the realm. I intend taking him back to London on the train before nightfall.'

'I acknowledge your concern, Mr Forbes, but I am investigating a serious case, sir. All I require is a few minutes with your suspect,' urged Ravenscroft.

Forbes thought deeply for a moment or two. 'Very well, Ravenscroft. I can give you half an hour, but I insist that I am present during your questioning, and that everything is conducted with the utmost secrecy.'

'Of course, Mr Forbes. Shall we adjourn to the police station?'

★   ★   ★

'So, Mr Flannigan, it seems that we have foiled your attempt to assassinate Lord Salisbury,' said Ravenscroft addressing the wounded gunman across the table.

The man remained silent, looking down at his tightly clasped hands on the table before him.

'It will do you no good to remain silent, my man. You have been caught red-handed trying to assassinate the Prime Minister of this country,' continued Ravenscroft. 'You know that your accomplice Murphy is dead?'

The man looked up briefly in surprise at Ravenscroft for a moment, before staring down at the floor.

'You might like to know how Murphy died. He was poisoned, but not before he had received a letter telling him to meet you here today at three o'clock. He was to be your fellow assassin. If your shot failed then possibly Murphy might have had greater success. Do you want to know who killed Murphy?'

'No concern of mine,' mumbled the man.

'Speak up, Flannigan,' urged Forbes seated at the corner of the table.

'I said it was no concern of mine,' snapped Flannigan.

'Do you know who poisoned him? Well I will tell you. Mr Cherrington, or rather Captain Quinton to give him his proper name. Is he a member of your so called brotherhood?' asked a hopeful Ravenscroft.

'Never heard of anyone called Quinton.'

'Oh, come now my man. The game is over. You will hang when my colleague here has finished with you. It will surely do your cause little harm to tell us about Quinton. Was he one of your members? Did he and Murphy have a falling out sometime in the past?' asked an anxious Ravenscroft knowing all too well that he was clutching at straws.

'I tell you I have never heard of this Quinton.'

'Shall I tell you what I think happened? I think Quinton killed Murphy to stop him talking. Come on, man, admit the truth. You know who this Quinton is,' said Ravenscroft raising his voice as he knew that he was getting nowhere, and that his time to question this man was quickly running out.

'I keep telling you, I don't know who this Quinton is,' retaliated Flannigan.

'And I tell you I think you are lying,' shouted Ravenscroft.

'Inspector, this is getting us nowhere,' interrupted Forbes.

'For goodness sake man, tell us what you know,' urged a desperate Ravenscroft.

'Go to the blazes!' growled Flannigan.

'That is all, inspector,' said Forbes standing up abruptly and looking at his pocket watch. 'If I am to get this man back to London tonight, I will need to leave now to catch the last train. I am afraid I cannot give you any more time. Men, put the cuffs on the prisoner and take him out of the room.'

'Just another few minutes,' pleaded Ravenscroft.

'I'm sorry, Ravenscroft,' said Forbes as Flannigan and the two policemen left the room. 'I will certainly let you know if we obtain any relevant information relating to your inquiries when we question Flannigan in London. I must say good day to you.'

Ravenscroft said nothing in reply as Forbes left the room.

'Damn it, Crabb, if only I could have had more time I'm sure we would have got the truth out of the man,' sighed Ravenscroft.

'Never mind, sir. At least we stopped the man killing the Prime Minister,' said Crabb attempting to break his superior's gloomy demeanour.

'I doubt we even did that. I have the distinct feeling that if we had not stopped that man Flannigan from firing his weapon then Forbes would have stepped in to save the situation, but I suppose we will never know one way or the other.'

'We still have Turco in custody sir.'

'You're right, Tom. I had almost forgotten about him. I wonder what he was doing here in Worcester today? I suppose he could be a part of all this?'

'Shall I go and fetch him, sir?'

'If you will.'

As Crabb closed the door behind him, Ravenscroft rose from his chair and began pacing up and down the room. It had been infuriating that he not been given more time to continue with his questioning of the Irish gunman. He kept telling himself that another hour would have secured not only a confession, but also a confirmation of Quinton's involvement and guilt, but all that had now been snatched away from him by Forbes and his special department at the Yard. Now he would be on his own once more, trying to discover the connection between the three men: Murphy, Flannigan and Quinton, and he was only too aware that time was rapidly running out. Tomorrow his chief suspect would be leaving Pershore, probably for good, and would be taking any solution to the case with him. All that remained now was the Italian musician, Turco. Would he provide the last minute evidence which Ravenscroft so badly needed?

The door suddenly opened and Turco and Crabb entered the room.

'What is-a this? Why have you done this to Turco?' cried the distressed man as he sat in the chair indicated by Crabb.

'What were you doing in Worcester today?' asked Ravenscroft resuming his seat and speaking directly at the man across the table.

'I was-a playing my beautiful violin for the people of Worcester,' replied Turco.

'Seemed more like begging to me,' muttered Crabb.

'No, no! Turco he no beg. He only play his fine melodies. Turco he needs people to listen.'

'Come now, Count, we saw the hat with the money at your feet. That is not the conduct of a famous violinist who gives recitals in the major concert halls of the land, but I don't believe that for one minute. Famous men such as that do not eek out a miserable life in a cheap lodging house in Pershore.'

'Maybe Turco he exaggerate. He sometime play in London,' admitted the embarrassed musician.

'And most days on the streets of Worcester?' suggested Ravenscroft. 'Unless of course that was just a deception.'

'A deception? I no understand.'

'Perhaps you are really a Fenian sympathiser, Count? Were you and Flannigan planning to assassinate the Prime Minister today?'

'I no understand. Who is this man Flannigan?' asked a puzzled Turco.

'Oh come now, Count. You know that Lord Salisbury was speaking here today, and that he is not in favour of Irish independence. That is why you and Flannigan planned to assassinate him, was it not?'

'What is this? Turco he no plan to kill anyone,' replied the alarmed violinist.

'The truth, man,' said Ravenscroft raising his voice. 'It looks bad for you. We know that Jones, or rather Murphy, was a member of the Fenian Brotherhood, and that together you were planning to join Flannigan in Worcester today to carry out your evil deed.'

'I do not understand any of this,' said Turco shaking his head and looking anxiously at Crabb as if he was expecting some help from that quarter.

'Don't deny it, Turco.'

'This is-a silly. Turco he is not a violent man. Turco he no want to kill anyone. Turco is a man of peace not war.'

'What I want to know is where does Mr Cherrington fit into all this? Was he once a member of your so called *brotherhood*? Did he and Murphy once argue and fall out? Did Murphy threaten to expose Cherrington? Is that why you and Cherrington decided to kill Murphy?' said Ravenscroft becoming more and more animated.

'Please, please!' said Turco crying into his hands.

'The truth, Turco!' demanded Ravenscroft slapping his hand down on the table. 'We want the truth! Come on, man!'

'Stop! Stop!' cried out Turco.

'Well?' demanded Ravenscroft.

'Yes, yes. Turco he no play in concert halls in London and other places. I earn my money by playing on the streets. What is-a wrong with that?' said the musician looking up at Ravenscroft with tears in his eyes.

'No, not that, man,' replied an irritated Ravenscroft. 'We want to know about you and Quinton, and Murphy.'

'I tell you I no understand. I have never

met either this Quinton or this Murphy before.'

'What was your part in this plot to kill the Prime Minister?' continued Ravenscroft becoming increasingly aware that he was not getting anywhere with his line of questioning, but being still reluctant to admit defeat.

'Plot? I know nothing of any plot. Please you let me go.'

'You will go when we have finished with you. Why don't you tell us all about your involvement in this plot. I am sure you will feel much better when you have told us everything,' urged Ravenscroft.

'I cannot tell you anything I do not know,' pleaded Turco.

'When did you meet Cherrington, or rather Quinton, before he came to Pershore?'

'I have-a never met this man before.'

'And Murphy?'

'I know no Murphy. Please, I have told you everything I know. You let Turco go now?'

'Were you having a relationship with Miss Martin?' asked Ravenscroft changing his line of questioning.

'No! The lady she no interested in Turco, and Turco he is only in love with his violin.'

'Did you kill her?'

'No! Turco he no kill.'

'Very well, Count. You are free to go,' said

Ravenscroft leaning back in his chair.

'Turco he go?' asked the perplexed musician.

'Yes, you may go.'

Turco looked across at Crabb as if expecting that the constable would march over to him at any moment and thrust his hands into the handcuffs, then he stared at Ravenscroft, who nodded, before rising from his chair and walking quickly out of the room.

'I don't think there was anything else to be gained,' sighed Ravenscroft. 'I believe him when he says that he was not part of this plot today.'

'Why, sir?' asked Crabb.

'You may recall that we found no weapon on him when we arrested him at the rally, and if Turco is a Fenian sympathizer then Forbes would probably have known that, and would have wanted to question him. The fact that Forbes showed no interest in Turco, and allowed us to question him on our own proves my point. Nevertheless I felt I had to push him on this matter, just in case.'

'He could still have met Murphy some time in the past.'

'Possibly, but again I think he was telling us the truth when he said he had never met Murphy or Quinton before they arrived at Talbots'.'

'So you don't think that Turco poisoned

either Jones or Miss Martin?'

'It looks that way. I had so hoped that Turco would have broken down and confessed all, but it seems that was a false hope. He will certainly have an interesting tale to relate to the others when he returns to Talbots' tonight.'

'What do we do now, sir?' asked Crabb.

'It's late, Tom. It has been a long day. Let us both go home. Tomorrow will be our last chance to arrest Quinton before he leaves the town, and who knows perhaps the mysterious Mr Claybourne might at last decide to make an appearance,' said Ravenscroft walking over to the door.

'Jenny says that you are to dine with us this evening, sir, and that if you refuses she will be most put out,' smiled Crabb.

'Then, Tom, it would be ungracious of me to refuse. It will be a pleasure to dine with you and your wife, and to see my little godson, Samuel again. Lead on Tom, I must admit that I have quite an appetite.'

13

Ledbury and Pershore

Ravenscroft pushed away his breakfast plate of bread and jam, and looked down again at the two opened letters that lay before him on the parlour table.

The first letter from Lucy telling of the family's adventures in Weymouth, and urging him to join them as soon as possible, had come as a welcome relief, but had also increased the frustration he felt that his latest case showed little signs of coming to a speedy conclusion. The events of the previous day, rather than offering a satisfactory end to the case, had only sought to cloud the issue even more.

The second letter had plunged him into despair. Written by Robertson in a shaky, sometimes incoherent hand, the words had come as a profound shock —

Ravenscroft,
It was good to see you yesterday.
After you left, I thought long and hard about your present case.
It has long been on my conscience all

these years that I may have caused an innocent man a grave injustice. When we arrested Quinton I was convinced that he had poisoned his wife, but the problem was that I was unable to prove it. Then I found the poor woman's diary. It was clear from reading its contents that the man she had married was a complete charlatan, who preyed on innocent women such as she was, to acquire their fortunes. I saw a way in which we could bring him to justice. I took the diary and wrote in the last entry telling how she knew that her husband was poisoning her. I knew that this was a wrong thing to have done, but I also realized that this would be the only way I could secure a conviction. We had not reckoned that Rawlinson would secure Quinton's release.

Now you have come face to face with the man again after all these years, and you, like me, believe in his guilt. I have long regretted my actions, and urge you now not to repeat my mistake, however desperate the situation may become. If you are tempted to tread along this path I believe you will regret it for the rest of your life. Do not let your eagerness to bring your case to a satisfactory conclusion cloud your judgement.

I now no longer know whether Quinton

did kill his wife or not.

I have lived with the result of my foolish actions for years. Now that I am about to die, I have felt the need to confess all to yourself.

I hope you can forgive me.

Please excuse my hand,

Your former colleague,
Robertson

Ravenscroft read the letter over again before burying his face in his hands. So Robertson had lied all those years ago. Anxious to secure a conviction he had manufactured the evidence. An innocent man could have been sent to the gallows, had it not been for the artful deliberations of Sefton Rawlinson Q.C. Worse still the lie, the deception, had been carried down the years, waiting for Ravenscroft to rekindle it in his present dealings with the man. Now his case lay in tatters. If Quinton had not poisoned his first wife then in all probability he had not poisoned Jones and Miss Martin either.

Ravenscroft acknowledged that he had pursued and hounded an innocent man, and that his prejudice and narrow mindedness had led to his present failure to solve the case. How could he have been so foolish?

★ ★ ★

'I suppose we will have to let him go,' said Crabb as he and Ravenscroft walked down the road towards the police station in Pershore.

'Yes, we have no reason to detain him,' replied an irritated Ravenscroft.

'He could still be our murderer,' suggested Crabb.

'If he didn't poison his first wife, what possible motive could he have for killing Jones and Miss Martin? There was nothing to conceal or protect.'

'I suppose you're right, sir. He could still have poisoned his wife in Pimlico. Just because Inspector Robertson wrote that false entry in the diary still doesn't mean that Quinton was innocent of that crime.'

'You could be right, but in view of Robertson's confession I feel that I have hounded the man too much,' admitted Ravenscroft.

'There could still be something in Quinton's past that we don't know about.'

'You mean that he and Jones, or rather Murphy, may have encountered each other many years ago?'

'Yes, sir.'

'To tell you the truth, Tom, I don't know what to believe any more. Perhaps I should resign from the case and let someone else

271

take over. I feel I have made too many mistakes,' said a gloomy Ravenscroft.

'By the time they send someone else out from Worcester, Quinton will have long left the town. I am sure something will happen soon to help us solve the case.'

'I wish I shared your optimism, Tom. Ah, here we are. Let's go and see if Hoskings has any news for us,' said Ravenscroft pushing open the door to the police station.

'No one here, sir,' remarked Crabb looking round the empty room.

'Hoskings! Hoskings,' shouted Ravenscroft.

The door to the inner room opened suddenly and the untidy, sleepy policeman rushed into the room.

'Good morning, sir,' stuttered Hoskings.

'Good grief man, have you been sleeping on the job?' asked an angry Ravenscroft.

'Sorry, sir. Sorry. It was the babby,' spluttered the constable hastily fastening the buttons of his tunic.

'What baby?' demanded Ravenscroft.

'Me and the wife. Babby kept us awake all night sir. Sorry, sir,' mumbled Hoskings.

'Hoskings, this will not do. I care little for you, or your wife, or your baby. Your duty is to remain presentable and alert in this station whilst on duty at all times,' said Ravenscroft.

'Yes, sir. Sorry, sir. It won't happen again, sir.'

'It had better not, Hoskings, or you will find yourself out on the street — and that will be no good to either your wife or your baby.'

'Yes, sir. I mean no, sir. Sorry, sir,' replied Hoskings busily tidying up the papers on the front desk.

'Well, Hoskings, has anything happened during our absence?' asked Ravenscroft in a quieter tone of voice, realizing that perhaps he had been a little unkind in his references to the policeman's offspring.

'Yes sir. A telegram arrived for you, sir, earlier this morning.'

'Yes man, where is it then?'

'It's here somewhere sir,' replied the unfortunate constable searching frantically through the collection of papers.

'For goodness sake, man,' moaned Ravenscroft.

'Here it is, sir,' said Hoskings retrieving an envelope and passing it over to Ravenscroft.

Ravenscroft tore open the envelope and studied the contents of the enclosed telegram.

'Anything important, sir?' asked Crabb after a few moments of silence had elapsed.

'It may be something, or nothing. Hoskings, give me pen and paper,' demanded Ravenscroft.

'Yes, sir.'

Ravenscroft wrote intently for a minute or two then passed over the paper to Hoskings.

'Take this to the telegraph office with all speed, and see that it is despatched to the address indicated straight away.'

'Yes, sir,' replied Hoskings picking up the paper and walking over to the door before pausing.

'Well man, why have you not gone?' asked Ravenscroft.

'Nearly forgot, sir. Someone was asking for you earlier this morning.'

'Yes, who was it?' asked an eager Ravenscroft.

'Can't remember his name, sir.'

'Perhaps it was Forbes come back again?' suggested Crabb.

'Well, Hoskings? If you can't remember his name, at least tell us what he looked like.'

'He was a youth, sir. About fourteen I would say. Said he knew you. Think he said his name was Stephens, or something like that.'

'Stebbins!' exclaimed Crabb.

'Yes that was it, sir. Stebbins that was his name. Cheeky young fellow,' said Hoskings.

'Did he say what he wanted?' enquired Ravenscroft.

'No, sir. Said he was going to see his girl over at Talbots', and that he would see you later, sir.'

'Right, Hoskings. You had better go now. And Hoskings?'

'Yes, sir?'

'With all speed if you will.'

'Yes, sir,' said the constable opening the door and leaving the station at a brisk pace.

'I wonder what Stebbins wanted?' said Crabb.

'Probably just curious to know how the case is progressing. If he comes back again tell him I am indisposed. The last thing I want this morning is Stebbins telling me how to conduct my affairs.'

'What was in the telegram, sir?' asked an inquisitive Crabb.

'Just another possible line of inquiry to follow. I will tell you about it later if it results in anything important.'

Suddenly the door was thrown open and a breathless Stebbins burst into the room.

'Good heavens, Stebbins, whatever is the matter?' asked Ravenscroft taken aback by the dramatic entrance of the young man.

'You has to come, sir,' panted Stebbins. 'She's dead!'

'Calm down, Stebbins,' instructed Ravenscroft.

'I tells you she's dead! At the bottom of the stairs. All in a heap!'

'Who is at the bottom of the stairs?' asked Crabb.

'That old woman. Miss Fanshaw. She's

dead as a cold cucumber. You has to come, Mr Ravenscroft. I tells you, she's dead!'

Ravenscroft and Crabb rushed out of the station and along the street, and pushed their way through the front entrance of Talbots' Lodging House, closely followed by an agitated Stebbins.

A group of figures — Maisie, Mrs Jacobson, Talbot, and Miss Arabella Fanshaw — could be seen clustered round a figure on the ground at the bottom of the stairs.

'Lord help us!' exclaimed Talbot looking wildly at the policemen.

Ravenscroft rushed over towards the body, and bending down on one knee examined it for any sign of life.

'Dead as a stuffed pheasant!' declared Stebbins attempting to gain a better view.

'Stebbins, be quiet!' reprimanded Ravenscroft. 'I am sorry, but Miss Fanshaw is dead.'

Miss Arabella Fanshaw let out a loud cry and looked as though she was going to faint.

'Perhaps you would be kind enough to take Miss Fanshaw back to her room, Maisie,' said an anxious Ravenscroft.

'Yes sir,' replied the maid placing a hand on the shoulder of the elderly sobbing woman and leading her gently back up the stairs.

'Talbot, I want you to go and fetch Doctor Homer as quickly as you can. Stebbins, you

276

can go with him,' instructed Ravenscroft.

The lodging-house keeper stared at Ravenscroft.

'Now man!' shouted Ravenscroft.

Talbot ran out of the house, closely followed by an eager Stebbins.

'How can it have happened?' asked Mrs Jacobson.

'That is what we intend to find out,' replied Ravenscroft.

'Rosanna, what has happened?' called out a voice from above.

'I must go to my husband, if you will excuse me?' said an agitated Mrs Jacobson.

'Yes, of course. That would be best,' replied Ravenscroft.

'Rosanna, where are you?' called the voice again.

Ravenscroft waited until Mrs Jacobson had climbed the stairs and returned to her room.

'She must have fallen all the way down the stairs, hitting her head on the floor here,' said Ravenscroft examining the corpse in more detail.

'The poor woman,' sympathized Crabb.

'Probably lost her footing, or she may have tripped over something on the landing. There is also the possibility that someone may have pushed her,' said Ravenscroft deep in thought.

'A little old lady like that. Who would want

her dead?' asked Crabb.

'I don't know, Tom. Perhaps Doctor Homer will be able to tell us more when he arrives with Talbot.'

'Must be very distressing for her sister.'

'Yes. The poor woman. In the meantime we must make sure that no one comes into the hallway here.'

★　★　★

'Well, Doctor, what can you tell us?' asked Ravenscroft after the body had been removed from Talbots' Lodging House.

'Very little, I am afraid. It is clear death was caused by a fall down the stairs. If you expect me to tell you whether she slipped of her own accord, or whether she was pushed, then I am afraid that you will be disappointed,' said Homer closing his medical bag.

'Thank you, Doctor Homer,' replied Ravenscroft.

'I have given Miss Arabella a sleeping draught. She has had a terrible shock. It would be better if she were not disturbed for the next few hours.'

'Of course.'

'Then I will take my leave, gentlemen. Good day to you both,' said Homer making his way out of the hall.

278

'We have already examined the top of the stairs. There is no obstacle there that could have caused a fall,' said Ravenscroft. 'She must have come down these same stairs twice or three times a day for the past ten years. Why did she slip today, I ask myself.'

'I reckon she was pushed,' said Crabb.

'Yes, but if that were the case, why was she pushed — and who pushed her?' asked Ravenscroft. 'I can see no reason why anyone would want the old woman dead, unless of course she had found out who the murderer of Jones and Miss Martin was, and that person decided to kill her before she could tell us.'

'Then her sister could also be in danger?'

'That could be the case, but I think it would be insensitive to interview the lady now. She is clearly distraught by the death of her sister, and as Homer said, should be left to sleep for the present. Well, Tom, this is a turn of events. What do you make of it? Accident or murder?'

'I still think she was pushed,' answered Crabb.

The door to the room opened and Stebbins peered round the edge of the woodwork.

'Not now, Stebbins. We are rather busy,' said Ravenscroft.

'It's Maisie, Mr Ravenscroft. She wants a word with you.'

'Is it important?'

'Yes sir,' replied Stebbins opening the door wider so that the maid could enter. 'Go on, Maisie my girl, you go and tell 'em what you saw.'

'All right Stebby, don't go on so,' said the maid entering the room.

'Maisie, how can we help you?' asked Ravenscroft.

'It's about Miss Clarisa.'

'Yes go on, Maisie,' urged Ravenscroft.

'Well sir, I may have seen something.'

'You saw what happened when Miss Fanshaw fell down the stairs?' asked Ravenscroft eagerly.

'Well, not exactly, sir. It was just after that, sir. I don't know if it is important, sir,' said the maid hesitantly.

'Go on, Maisie.'

'I was in the kitchen at the time, then I heard this loud noise like someone or something falling down the stairs, so I rushed into the hall, saw it was Miss Clarisa, and then I looked upwards.'

'You saw someone else on the landing?'

'Yes, sir. I saw Professor Jacobson disappearing into his room.'

'You saw Professor Jacobson?' asked Ravenscroft.

'Yes, sir. I just caught sight of the back of

his old jacket as the door closed.'

'But you didn't actually see him push Miss Fanshaw down the stairs?'

'No, sir.'

'You are absolutely certain on this point. You did not actually see Miss Fanshaw fall down the stairs, but you did see Professor Jacobson disappearing into his room?'

'Yes, sir. Did I do right in telling you this, sir?' asked the maid.

'Yes, Maisie. You did the correct thing. Thank you.'

'Told you Mr Ravenscroft would want to know everything, me girl. Reckon that old boy threw her off the landing,' said a cheery Stebbins.

'You don't know that at all, Stebbins.'

'You going to question him then, Mr Ravenscroft?'

'Yes, Stebbins. May I suggest that you take Maisie back to the kitchen. You can see that she is somewhat distressed by this event,' suggested Ravenscroft.

'Right you are, Mr Ravenscroft. You come with me, old girl,' replied the young man placing his arm round the young maid's shoulder and leading her out of the room.

'Well, that's a surprise,' remarked Crabb.

'Yes, I think we should go and question the professor without delay.'

'Come in, gentlemen, we were expecting you,' said Rosanna opening the door so that the two detectives could enter.

'Thank you, Mrs Jacobson. Professor,' said Ravenscroft addressing the old man seated by the fireplace.

'This is a sad business. Poor Miss Fanshaw,' said Jacobson.

'Indeed, sir. When I entered just now Mrs Jacobson, you remarked that you were expecting us. Why was that?' asked Ravenscroft eagerly.

'You know that my husband was on the landing when Miss Fanshaw fell?' said Rosanna.

'The maid told us,' replied Ravenscroft.

'My wife had just gone into the room. I was following on behind when I heard this great noise,' began Jacobson.

'My husband drew my attention to what had just happened. I immediately turned round and rushed out on the landing where I saw Miss Fanshaw at the bottom of the stairs,' added Rosanna.

'Forgive me, I do not quite understand. You were both going into your room, Mrs Jacobson first, with you Professor behind, when you heard the sound of Miss Fanshaw falling?' asked Ravenscroft.

'That is correct, inspector,' replied the old man.

'When you were on the landing did you see anyone else there before you entered your room, Mrs Jacobson?'

'No. There was no one there.'

'And did you hear anything, Professor?'

'I heard the sound of a door closing. Most likely Miss Fanshaw's room.'

'And then?' urged Ravenscroft.

'I assumed that someone had just come out of the room. Then I heard this sound, like someone falling.'

'And what did you do next, sir?'

'I stood still for a moment, trying to ascertain what had happened. I called out, but no one replied, so I came into this room and told Rosanna what I had just heard.'

'I see,' said Ravenscroft looking at the old man and trying to work out whether he was telling the truth. 'Tell me, professor, when you were on the landing did you hear any other movement?'

'I do not understand, inspector?'

'When you heard the fall, were you aware of anyone else on the landing?'

The old man thought carefully for a moment before answering. 'No, I do not think there was anyone else there.'

'Thank you,' said Ravenscroft.

'I know what you are thinking, inspector. You are a policeman. I have known policemen in St. Petersburg. They all think alike. You think that I pushed Miss Fanshaw down the stairs?' said Jacobson.

Ravenscroft said nothing.

'I see,' smiled Jacobson. 'You will not say because you do not know. Perhaps I can help you, inspector? Ask yourself, why would I have wanted to kill Miss Fanshaw in such a dreadful fashion? I am blind, inspector. I would not have seen the good lady. Neither my wife nor I had any cause to hurt Miss Fanshaw. We have all lived under this roof, together, for the past five years. If either of us had wanted to harm the lady do you not think that we would have done the deed before now?'

'Perhaps Miss Fanshaw knew who had poisoned Mr Jones and Miss Martin,' suggested Ravenscroft.

'And you think that person was either my wife or I?'

'I would not like to say,' replied Ravenscroft only too aware that he was no longer asking the questions.

'I can assure you, inspector, that we are both completely innocent regarding this incident. I am sorry if we have disappointed you,' said Jacobson drawing the shawl closer round his person.

'I think we have answered all your

284

questions, inspector,' said Rosanna. 'If you will excuse us, my husband needs his rest.'

'Of course. Thank you both for your information. Good day to you.'

★ ★ ★

'He was very sure of himself,' said Crabb as he and Ravenscroft closed the front door of Talbots' behind them.

'Yes, it was almost as though he and his wife had rehearsed what they were going to tell us. It was all too neat and tidy for my liking, but I suppose it could be the truth.'

'Ah, Ravenscroft!' exclaimed a familiar figure walking briskly towards them.

'Mr Quinton,' acknowledged Ravenscroft.

'What brings you back to Talbots'? I trust you have caught the real criminal this time?' said Quinton with a note of sarcasm in his voice.

'You have evidently not heard, sir.'

'Heard what?'

'That Miss Clarisa Fanshaw is dead,' answered Ravenscroft.

'Good grief!'

'She was found at the bottom of the stairs, just over an hour ago. Where were you then, Mr Quinton?'

'Now look here, Ravenscroft, this will not

do at all. If you must know I have been out walking for the past two hours. Thought I would have a last look at the place before I left this evening. What a terrible business. Was the poor woman pushed, or did she fall?' asked Quinton casually.

'We are not sure at present. In view of this tragic situation, I would be obliged if you would delay your departure for London.'

'Sorry old boy. Train goes at seven this evening. Can't oblige, I'm afraid,' smiled Quinton turning away and walking up to the front door.

'Insufferable man!' exclaimed Ravenscroft as he and Crabb continued with their walk. 'He knows perfectly well that we cannot detain him, and obviously delights in our failure to do so.'

★   ★   ★

'Well, Tom, I can think of no solution to this mystery. Can you?'

It was later that afternoon, and Ravenscroft and Crabb were seated in one of the local hostelries partaking of their third tankard of ale.

'No, sir, but I still think it was that awful Quinton who did away with them all,' returned Crabb.

'I suppose he could have left the house, then slipped back later unobserved, and waited for Miss Clarisa to come out onto the landing, before pushing her down the stairs and then affecting his escape whilst everyone else was distracted. I cannot see that however. Firstly the Jacobsons noticed no one on the landing when they came up the stairs, and secondly how would Quinton have known that Miss Fanshaw was about to step out onto the landing and that she would have been alone? Also if he was leaving Pershore tonight why would he have bothered to have killed the old lady at all? No, I cannot see Quinton having anything to do with Miss Clarisa's death.'

'What about the Jacobsons? Their room is directly opposite the Misses Fanshaw. They could have waited for her to come out of the room, pushed her down the stairs, and then concocted their story,' suggested Crabb.

'Yes, that could be so, but again how would they know that Miss Clarisa would have been alone at that time? No, none of it seems to fit. Of course there is the obvious solution, that she tripped and fell. In which case her death was entirely accidental, and we have no case to investigate,' said a resigned Ravenscroft.

The door of the inn suddenly opened and a breathless Constable Hoskings rushed into the room. 'Ah, there you are, sir. I've been looking for you all round the town.'

'We did tell you, Hoskings, where we would be,' replied Ravenscroft taking another mouthful of ale.

'Oh yes, sir. I forgot. Sorry, sir,' said the apologetic policeman.

'Yes, well what is it, Hoskings?' asked an irritated Ravenscroft.

'Yes, sir. Sorry, sir. This telegram came for you,' said the constable producing a crumpled envelope from his pocket and attempting to smooth out the creases.

Ravenscroft tore open the envelope and studied the contents of the telegram.

'Good heavens! This changes everything, Tom.'

'What is it, sir?'

'A reply to my inquiry of earlier today. It seems that we have been following the wrong path. Of course, I see it all now!' exclaimed Ravenscroft. 'Come on, Tom. I think it is time we made an arrest!'

14

Pershore

Ravenscroft looked across at the assembled group of people seated around the table in the dining room of Talbots' Lodging House. Jacobson was staring out vacantly before him, his arm gripped tightly by his anxious wife; Quinton sitting back in his chair with his usual air of casual indifference; a red-eyed Arabella Fanshaw staring down at her hands tightly clutching the handkerchief on her lap; Turco, the violinist moving uneasily in his chair whilst drumming his fingers impatiently on the table; Maisie the maid, biting one of her fingernails whilst staring vaguely down at the floor, and Talbot himself looking furtively around the room whilst his large wife sat immobile and seemed to tower over the landlord. Ravenscroft knew that if he presented his case well then within the next few minutes he would be successful in obtaining a full confession from one of the gathering.

'Thank you, Constable Crabb, I think we are all here now, so you may close the door,' said Ravenscroft taking up his position before the spluttering flames in the fireplace.

Crabb closed the door and he and Hoskings then took up their places at the entrance to the room.

'Aren't you forgetting one thing, Ravenscroft?' said Quinton.

'Oh, and what might that be, sir?'

'Well, we are not, as you say, all here. You are forgetting Claybourne.'

'As Mr Claybourne is not here to join us, Captain Quinton, then I believe we must proceed without him,' replied Ravenscroft.

Quinton shrugged his shoulders and looked away.

'Here, who's this Quinton? I thought his name was Cherrington,' said Talbot.

'All will be revealed, my dear sir. When I first came to this house to investigate the death of Mr Jones I was not quite certain what I would find. Here was a man who had been with you for fewer than two weeks, who appeared to be unknown to all of you, and who had apparently died in his sleep after drinking too much Brown Windsor soup, only of course we all now know that that was not the real cause of his death. He had in fact been the victim of some kind of poison, which had been placed by someone in his tawny port; a suspicion that was later corroborated when we discovered that the bottle in question had been removed from this room, in all likelihood, by the person who had perpetrated the deed. When we tried to find out more about the deceased man we had little to help us, nothing of a personal nature, only a fragment from a letter. Even the corpse itself had been buried before our arrival and, although we later recovered the dead man's pocket watch and pistol, these items added little to what we knew about him — besides revealing their owner's real name to be Charles Murphy. Later we discovered that this Murphy had been a member of the Fenian Brotherhood, and that he had been sent to this area to await instructions to assassinate Lord Salisbury, the Prime Minister, at a meeting in Worcester.'

'We would not have let him in through the door, had we known what he was,' interrupted Mrs Talbot disapprovingly.

'The question is, though, had Murphy discovered something of vital importance during his short stay here, or was he already known to one of you here present? Then we turn to Miss Martin. Why was she poisoned? I believe she knew who had poisoned Jones, and that she was blackmailing that person, seeing it as an opportunity to escape the life of near penury in which she had lived here. Like Keats's nightingale she sought a better life for herself, but of course that life was cruelly cut short. So we return to Jones, or rather Murphy. He must be the answer to this mystery. One of you here had encountered the man, somewhere, and at some time in the past — but who? As we began to inquire further we found that this was a house of secrets, where everyone it seemed was not who he, or she, appeared to be, and where each of you had a secret to hide.'

Ravenscroft paused for a moment and observed that all his suspects had looked away from him, each anxious to avoid his gaze.

'Count Turco, the eminent concert violinist, but it was clear to me that such claims of fame were entirely fabricated — '

'You call Turco a liar?' retorted the musician jumping up out of his seat. 'Turco, he is very famous in Naples and Capri. People there they queue to hear the great Turco!'

'That's as may be, Count, but a famous concert violinist has no need to live out a meagre existence in a cheap lodging house in Pershore, or to play his violin on the streets of Worcester,' continued Ravenscroft. 'I would be obliged, sir, if you would regain your seat.'

Turco sat down muttering as he did so.

'The question is — could you, Count, and

our friend Jones have met somewhere in the past? Then there is you, Professor Jacobson. I wonder if you and Jones met in St. Petersburg? And what was the real reason for your leaving there?'

'I have told you why I left, inspector,' answered the old man. 'It is not my fault if you cannot accept what I have told you. And I certainly never encountered Mr Jones there or anywhere else.'

'Then we come to Mrs Jacobson, who was anxious to hide from us her true status whilst living in London. Could Jones have been one of her former clients, threatening to expose her past to everyone here, and that was why he had to be silenced?'

'That is all nonsense,' replied Mrs Jacobson.

'I wonder if your husband knows where you go on certain afternoons?' continued Ravenscroft.

'Rosanna, what does he mean?' asked Jacobson anxiously.

'It is nothing, my dear, I will tell you later. It is past now,' said the old man's wife staring intently at Ravenscroft.

'Did you know, professor, that your wife and Mr Claybourne had taken out a life insurance policy on your life, and that she had recently purchased a quantity of arsenic powder from the local chemist's?'

'Yes of course,' laughed Jacobson. 'The policy is to provide some security for Rosanna in the event of my death.'

'Told you it was that fellow Claybourne, but you would not listen, Ravenscroft,' said Quinton with an air of confidence.

'Now let us turn to you, Mr Talbot,' said Ravenscroft turning to face the landlord.

'Now look here, we had nothing to do with this business,' protested Talbot.

'A man of many secrets,' continued Ravenscroft, ignoring the outburst, 'prone to exaggeration and deceitfulness. It was you who concealed the vital items of the dead man from us, thereby hindering our investigations. I also don't believe you were ever in the Crimea.'

'Told you, Talbot, we should have got rid of that picture long ago,' interrupted the landlady.

'Always seeking to cover up some assignation or other. I wondered whether you had met Jones long ago, and whether some untold criminal act had been committed then, an act that Jones now sought to expose?'

'Poppycock!' snapped Talbot.

'And so we turn to you, Mister Cherrington, or should I say Quinton, as that of course is your real name, always seeking to hide the truth from us about your former lives in Pimlico and India. Could you have met Jones long ago, and did he know your secret, and was that why he had to be silenced?'

'Nonsense, all of it nonsense. It is time I left. My train departs in just over an hour. I have heard enough,' said Quinton rising from the table. 'You clearly have nothing, Ravenscroft.'

'But there you are wrong, captain. I now know everything. If you will resume your seat, I will not detain you for very much longer,' replied Ravenscroft as Crabb took a step forwards.

Quinton stared at Crabb. 'Oh, very well then. I suppose a few more minutes won't matter.'

'Thank you, captain. As we continued with our investigations we encountered one lie after another, and there was always one more deception to be revealed. I realized that if we were ever to obtain the truth about this matter, then I would need to know as much as I could about the deceased man. Who was this Jones or Murphy? We now know he was one of the Fenians, and like most members of the infamous Brotherhood he must have originated from Ireland. What had he left behind for us? The scrap of paper giving us the date and time of the important meeting in Worcester, the pocket watch which had revealed his real name, and the weapon which he intended using in his assassination attempt. It was finally the gun itself that was to reveal the answer to all these crimes.'

'Go on, Ravenscroft,' said Quinton leaning forwards. 'This is all most intriguing.'

'The gun revealed the name of its maker — 'John Elliott'. Who was this 'John Elliot?' In order to answer this question, I sent a telegram to a colleague of mine at the firearms department of the British Museum. He was able to provide me with details of the maker. John Elliott was a gunmaker in Coleraine in northern Ireland.'

'Still don't see where all this is leading,' interjected Quinton.

'Coleraine. That was where Murphy originated. Then I remembered a story that had been told me by one of those present now, when I looked at a portrait of a young boy, who had died over twenty years ago in Coleraine. And so I decided to investigate further, and have today received a reply from my colleagues in the Special Branch at the Home Office,' said Ravenscroft removing the crumpled telegram from his pocket. 'I will read what it says. Or would you like to tell us, Miss Fanshaw, how once, long ago, your late brother and Mr Murphy had been business partners in Coleraine, and how Murphy was responsible for your brother's untimely death. How you and your sister were then forced to sell the family estate to pay off the debts, and how eventually you came here to Pershore, where you lived in quiet seclusion, until one day a stranger arrived calling himself Jones. He did not recognize you of course, having never met you in person whilst in Coleraine, although the name must have been familiar. You remembered him, without doubt, as the man who had caused your brother's death, and so you decided — '

'All right, inspector, there is no need to go on with all this,' interrupted Arabella. 'Yes, I poisoned that evil man who had destroyed my brother.'

'Lord above!' exclaimed Talbot.

'I should have realized earlier, all those unanswered questions whenever your sister wanted to tell us more about your life in Ireland, and how you were always so protective towards her. Why did you then poison Miss Martin? She surely did not deserve to die?' asked Ravenscroft.

'She saw me removing the bottle from this room, the morning after, and realized that we had poisoned that man. She thought she could extract money from us to buy her silence, but I realized that if we complied with her request she would only come back for more.'

'And so you entered her room, when she was absent, and added poison to her drink. You were careful not to purchase any poisons locally, which would have aroused suspicion,' said Ravenscroft.

Arabella said nothing as she stared down at her hands twisting the handkerchief between her fingers.

'Poor Miss Clarisa,' said an ashen-faced Maisie.

'Lords! She must have thrown her down the stairs as well!' exclaimed Talbot suddenly realizing the seriousness of the disclosures.

'I do not think so,' said Ravenscroft. 'I believe that Miss Clarisa realized that once we had apprehended Flannigan in Worcester it would only be a matter of time before we discovered that the dead man here had originated from Coleraine, and that our investigations in that area would enable us to arrive at the truth. Rather than face the outcome, I believe that Miss Clarisa decided — '

'Poor Clarisa', interjected Arabella. 'We knew that you would be coming for us, and she could not bear the outcome.'

'Although of course, it may have been a simple accident,' continued Ravenscroft. 'I do not think that it will ever be possible to know.'

'You English, you always do these things in such a quiet dignified manner,' muttered Turco.

'Hoskings, call in the other officers outside and then take Miss Fanshaw back to the station if you will,' instructed Ravenscroft.

Arabella rose from her seat as the constable stepped forwards removing the handcuffs from his belt.

'There will be no need for those, Hoskings. I am sure Miss Fanshaw has no intention of escaping.'

'Thank you, inspector. My brother committed suicide you know because of that evil man and the ruin he brought on our family. He did not deserve that. You may do as you wish with me. I am content now that my brother has at last obtained justice,' said Arabella directly addressing Ravenscroft.

Ravenscroft gave a slight bow as Arabella followed Hoskings out of the room.

'Well, that's a fine turn of events,' remarked Quinton.

'Poor Miss Fanshaw,' said Maisie crying out loud.

'For goodness sake, girl, pull yourself together,' reprimanded Mrs Talbot.

'How sad,' said Jacobson shaking his head from side to side.

'Yes, professor, you are correct, it is a very

sad case indeed,' said Ravenscroft.

'One good thing, though. If the old ladies had not poisoned old Murphy, then you would not have come here, and the Prime Minster would have been dead by now,' offered Quinton.

Ravenscroft allowed himself a brief smile, before addressing the group for the final time. 'Well, ladies and gentlemen, now that our work here is concluded, Constable Crabb and I will take our leave.'

'What will happen to Miss Fanshaw?' asked Rosanna.

'Constable Crabb and I will return to the station where we will take Miss Fanshaw's statement, after which she will be formally charged with the deaths of Charles Murphy and Miss Martin. She will then be taken to the gaol in Worcester where she will reside until her trial. Now, we will take our leave. Good day to you all. I wonder if I might have a private word with you, sir?' said Ravenscroft addressing Quinton.

'Yes. Yes of course.'

Ravenscroft, Crabb and Quinton stepped out into the hall and closed the door to the dining room behind them.

'Captain Quinton, it seems that I owe you an apology. Because of your involvement in the Pimlico Poisoning Case all those years ago, I let that case deeply influence my investigations in this affair, to the extent that I, wrongly as it turned out, thought that you were the guilty party in this matter,' began Ravenscroft somewhat hesitatingly, looking for the correct words to use.

'Go on,' said Quinton intently.

'New evidence has recently come to light that proves your innocence in the Pimlico case. It seems that your wife did not write those last words in the diary shortly before her death, in which she accused you of poisoning her.'

'I see. Then who did?'

'I am afraid that I am not at liberty to say. Fortunately justice was done at the time and you were rightfully acquitted. It seems that Mr Sefton Rawlinson was defending an innocent man,' continued Ravenscroft feeling embarrassed and ill at ease as he continued. 'When I realized that you were really Quinton and not Cherrington, I was sure that you were concealing more than a change of identity from us, and I now accept that I was somewhat over-zealous in my questioning. I now know that my suspicions were unfounded and misguided, and I trust that you will do me the courtesy, sir, in accepting my profound and sincere apologies for any distress we, I mean I, may have caused you.'

'Well yes, I suppose so,' replied Quinton somewhat at a loss for words.

'Then will you give me your hand, sir?' asked Ravenscroft.

'Of course. No harm done, old boy,' replied Quinton taking the extended hand and shaking it.

'I thank you, sir,' said a relieved Ravenscroft.

'You know one thing, Ravenscroft? I really did love my wife, you must believe that.'

'Yes, captain, I believe what you say, but I must not detain you. I believe you have a train to catch to London?'

'Yes. No hurry now though, I suppose. Might as well stay on for a day or so in Pershore. I am quite fond of the town really. This was where I first met my wife you know.'

'Yes sir, I know. Then we wish you a good day, Captain Quinton, and please accept our best wishes for the future.'

Ravenscroft and Crabb stepped outside, closing the door behind them.

'Well, Tom, that's an end to the case. Let us go and take Miss Fanshaw's statement, then you and Hoskings can convey her to Worcester.'

'Fancy there is still a chance of a few days in Weymouth,' smiled Crabb.

'Indeed, Tom. Yes indeed. There was a time

when I thought that we would never solve this case, but I do not think we should linger under that swinging sign any longer. It looks even more precarious than usual.'

As Ravenscroft and Crabb walked down the path they suddenly collided with a short, stocky, dark-haired man who had just turned the corner.

'My dear sir. Please accept my apologies,' said Ravenscroft.

'Should have looked where you were going', snapped the new arrival. 'You just come from Talbots'?'

'Yes — and you must be Mr Claybourne, if I am not mistaken?' asked Ravenscroft.

'Yes — and who the devil are you?' growled the man.

'Ravenscroft. Inspector Ravenscroft — and this is my colleague, Constable Crabb.'

'Police. What the deuce has been going on whilst I have been away?' asked Claybourne.

'Oh a great deal Mr Claybourne, a great deal, but everything is now resolved. I am sure Mr Talbot will be able to tell you all about it.'

'Suppose that will have to do then. Good day to you,' replied Claybourne abrupty.

'Good day to you as well, sir.'

Ravenscroft and Crabb watched as the man walked briskly down the front path and in through the front entrance, slamming the door behind him as he did so.

'So we meet the elusive Mr Claybourne at last,' said Ravenscroft as he and Crabb turned to go.

Suddenly a large crashing sound rang out behind them.

The two men turned to see that the sign above the doorway of the lodging house had landed on the ground near the front entrance of the building.

Ravenscroft laughed. 'I would say that was rather a fitting end to everything. Would you not agree, Tom?'

Epilogue

Pershore, the Next Day

She entered the abbey, somewhat apprehensively, as the rain blew across the grounds of the imposing building, and was grateful to find the building empty, so that she could be alone with her thoughts.

She stood there for some moments admiring the fine window that looked down across the nave.

'There are no monks here now.'

The unexpected voice startled her, and she let out a cry and dropped her umbrella as she turned round to see who had broken the silence of the church.

'My dear good lady. Do please forgive me,' said the stranger bending down and retrieving the umbrella. 'I should not have spoken out and alarmed you in such a manner.'

'I did not think there was anyone here,' she replied attempting to recover her composure.

'Permit me,' said the tall bearded stranger handing the umbrella back to its owner, with a smile, before removing his hat and giving a slight bow.

'Thank you,' she said turning away.

'All the monks left hundreds of years ago, I believe. Something to do with Henry VIII. Dissolution of the monasteries, and all that. It was much larger than this in medieval times I understand.'

'You seem remarkably well informed, sir. You are a resident of this town?' she asked, making polite conversation, whilst seeking to leave as soon as possible.

'Good lord no. Just staying here for a few days on my way up to London. May I be so bold as to ask if you are a visitor to the town?'

'My aunt and I are staying at the Angel.'

'A good choice, I believe.'

'My father has recently died,' she began not knowing why she should have uttered those words to a complete stranger, and feeling the tears beginning to well up in her eyes.

'My good lady, I am so sorry. I would not have asked had I known. Please take this,' said the stranger showing concern as he passed over a large handkerchief.

'You are most kind, sir. Please forgive me. It is all so recent,' she replied drying her eyes on the handkerchief.

'Of course. I sympathize with your plight. My dear wife, whom I worshipped above all others, has also recently passed away,' said the man turning away.

'Then you know,' she began to hand back the handkerchief.

'Please accept it with my compliments. They say that time is a healer, but I am not quite so sure. What would you say?' he said looking sadly into her eyes.

'I suppose we must all have faith.'

'You are so right, my good lady. Without faith there cannot be hope, and we all need hope if we are ever to obtain happiness.'

She forced a smile, thinking the stranger's words both eloquent and heartfelt.

'I believe the rain may have ceased,' he said. 'May I escort you back to the Angel?' smiled the man.

'That is most kind of you, sir.'

'In fact there is something which you may be able to assist me with — no, sorry, I have been far too bold.'

'What is it, sir?'

'Well, I find myself in something of a difficulty. I have today received a communication from an elderly aunt of mine who wishes me to purchase a box of lace handkerchiefs for her. Now, I must admit that I have very little taste when it comes to choosing lace handkerchiefs for elderly maiden aunts,' laughed the man. 'I wonder whether you could assist me in my choice? There is a good shop I believe halfway down the main street.

No, I am sorry, I have been too forthright in my request. You must forgive me.'

'I would be happy to assist you, sir, in your quest.'

'That is most uncommonly good of you, my dear lady. Perhaps you would care to accompany me there, but I fear I have been somewhat remiss. I should introduce myself. My name is Cherrington. Charles Cherrington,' smiled the stranger.

'I am pleased to make your acquaintance, Mr Cherrington,' she replied.

'Then shall we begin, my good lady? The world awaits us.'

We do hope that you have enjoyed reading this large print book.

Did you know that all of our titles are available for purchase?

We publish a wide range of high quality large print books including:
Romances, Mysteries, Classics
General Fiction
Non Fiction and Westerns

Special interest titles available in large print are:
The Little Oxford Dictionary
Music Book
Song Book
Hymn Book
Service Book

Also available from us courtesy of Oxford University Press:
Young Readers' Dictionary
(large print edition)
Young Readers' Thesaurus
(large print edition)

For further information or a free brochure, please contact us at:
Ulverscroft Large Print Books Ltd.,
The Green, Bradgate Road, Anstey,
Leicester, LE7 7FU, England.
Tel: (00 44) 0116 236 4325
Fax: (00 44) 0116 234 0205

Other titles published by Ulverscroft:

THE DROITWICH DECEIVERS

Kerry Tombs

April 1890. Whilst visiting a local church-yard, the nine-year-old daughter of a prominent Droitwich businessman disappears without a trace. Detective Inspector Ravenscroft and his colleague, Constable Tom Crabb, investigate. Then, in a seemingly unconnected incident, Ravenscroft's wife, Lucy, is asked by a distraught mother to find the baby that she'd been compelled to give away. As the investigations proceed, both Ravenscroft and Lucy encounter the darkened world of Victorian child exploitation: lies, deceit and murder are commonplace — and they are stuck in a desperate race against time to save the endangered children . . .